**Praise for Rose Pressey
and her delightful HAUNTED VINTAGE mysteries**

"Rose Pressey's books are fun!"
—*New York Times* best-selling author
Janet Evanovich

IF YOU'VE GOT IT, HAUNT IT
"A delightful protagonist, intriguing twists, and a
fashionista ghost combine in a hauntingly fun
tale. Definitely haute couture."
—*New York Times* best-selling author
Carolyn Hart

"If you're a fan of vintage clothing and quirky
ghosts, Rose Pressey's *If You've Got It, Haunt It* will
ignite your passion for fashion and pique your
otherworldly interest. Wind Song, the enigmatic
cat, adds another charming layer to the mystery."
—*New York Times* best-selling author
Denise Swanson

"*If You've Got It, Haunt It* is a stylish mystery full of
vintage fashions and modern flair, with a dash of
Rose Pressey's trademark paranormal wit for that
final touch of panache. Chic and quirky heroine
Cookie Chanel and a supporting cast of small-
town Southern characters are sure to charm
lovers of high fashion and murderous hi-jinks
alike."
—*New York Times* and *USA Today* best-selling
author **Jennie Bentley**

"Absolutely delightful! Prolific author Rose Pressey has penned a delightful mystery full of Southern charm, vintage fashion tips, a ghostly presence, and a puzzler of a mystery. With snappy dialogue and well-drawn characters in a lovely small-town setting, this thoroughly engaging story has it all."
—*New York Times* **best-selling author Jenn McKinlay**

"Fun, fast-paced, and fashionable, *If You've Got It, Haunt It* is the first in Rose Pressey's appealing new mystery series featuring clever vintage-clothing expert Cookie Chanel. A charming Southern setting, an intriguing murder, a stylish ghost, a tarot-reading cat, and a truly delectable detective combine to make Ms. Pressey's new Haunted Vintage series a sheer delight."
—*New York Times* **best-selling author Kate Carlisle**

"Prolific mystery author Pressey launches a cozy alternative to Terri Garey's 'Nicki Styx' series with an appealing protagonist who is as sweet as a Southern accent. The designer name-dropping and shopping tips from Cookie add allure for shopaholics."
—*Library Journal*

IF THE HAUNTING FITS, WEAR IT
"Cookie Chanel must investigate the horse-racing community to find a killer. . . . After *Haunted Is Always in Fashion*, Pressey's fifth amusing paranormal cozy is filled with quirky characters and fash-

ion, along with a few ghosts. Fans of Juliet Blackwell's 'Witchcraft' mysteries may enjoy the vintage clothing references. Suggest also for fans of Tonya Kappes."
—*Library Journal*

"Haunted by three ghosts, a young woman searches for a jockey's murderer at the Kentucky Derby."
—*Kirkus Reviews*

HAUNT COUTURE AND GHOSTS GALORE
"It was a pleasure to read. I listened to this one, and I'm so glad I did. The novel is narrated by Tara Ochs. She does a fine job of narrating, keeping up the pace and differentiating voices well. The story moved right along. If you have a chance to listen, I recommend it with this one."
—**Jaquo.com** (on the audio edition)

FASHIONS FADE, HAUNTED IS ETERNAL
"Chock full of ghosts, supernatural guardians, cats possessed by spirits, a handsome police officer boyfriend, and tips on surviving the afterlife and vintage shopping."
—*Kirkus Reviews*

Books by Rose Pressey

The Haunted Craft Fair Mystery Series
Murder Can Mess Up Your Masterpiece
Murder Can Confuse Your Chihuahua

The Haunted Vintage Mystery Series
If You've Got It, Haunt It
All Dressed Up and No Place to Haunt
Haunt Couture and Ghosts Galore
If the Haunting Fits, Wear It
Haunted Is Always in Fashion
A Passion for Haunted Fashion
Fashions Fade, Haunted Is Eternal

The Haunted Tour Guide Mystery Series
These Haunts Are Made for Walking
Walk on the Haunted Side
Haunt the Haunt, Walk the Walk
Walk This Way, Haunt This Way
Take a Haunted Walk with Me
Hauntin' After Midnight
Keep on Haunting
You'll Never Haunt Alone
The Walk That Haunts Me

The Halloween LaVeau Series
Forever Charmed
Charmed Again
Third Time's a Charm
Charmed, I'm Sure
A Charmed Life
Charmed Ever After
Once Upon a Charmed Time
Charmed to Death
A Charmed Cauldron
Almost Charmed

MURDER
Can Confuse
Your Chihuahua

Rose Pressey

KENSINGTON BOOKS
www.kensingtonbooks.com

KENSINGTON BOOKS are published by

Kensington Publishing Corp.
119 West 40th Street
New York, NY 10018

All Kensington titles, imprints, and distributed lines are available at special quantity discounts for bulk purchases for sales promotion, premiums, fund-raising, educational, or institutional use.

Special book excerpts or customized printings can also be created to fit specific needs. For details, write or phone the office of the Kensington Sales Manager: Attn.: Sales Department. Kensington Publishing Corp., 119 West 40th Street, New York, NY 10018. Phone: 1-800-221-2647.

Kensington and the K logo Reg. U.S. Pat. & TM Off.

First Printing: May 2020
ISBN-13: 978-1-4967-2163-1
ISBN-10: 1-4967-2163-2

ISBN-13: 978-1-4967-2164-8 (ebook)
ISBN-10: 1-4967-2164-0 (ebook)

10 9 8 7 6 5 4 3 2 1

Printed in the United States of America

To my parents, for always being there for me. You've inspired me with your strength, love, and kindness. I'm proud to call you Mom and Dad.

CHAPTER 1

Don't worry if you don't sell a lot at your first craft fair. Focus more on building relationships and having fun, plus staying alive.

How would I escape this? I was trapped with no idea how to get out. Where was help when I needed it? My heart rate spiked while my body trembled. With shaky hands, I gripped the steering wheel of my 1947 pink Ford F-100 truck. I punched the gas pedal, hoping to flee before anyone noticed. Unfortunately, the wheels spun, but the truck, with my pink and white Shasta trailer attached to the back, went nowhere. As I gunned the engine, I wondered if I'd cause irreversible damage.

Vincent van Gogh, my tiny white Chihuahua, sat on the seat next to me. He barked as if telling me I was doing this all wrong.

"I know, Van, but what else can I do?" I pressed my foot on the pedal again.

Obviously, I'd named Van after the famed artist. It wasn't entirely because of my love of art either. I'd rescued the Chihuahua from the shelter a year ago, and his one floppy ear had inspired the name. We'd been best friends ever since. Van was opinionated, though, and always let me know when I wasn't doing something to his satisfaction.

Bearing down on the accelerator again resulted in the same outcome. What else was I supposed to do? A tow truck seemed like my only option. I'd been so close to arriving at my destination, only to be stopped a short distance away. The spot where I'd set up my booth for the craft fair came into view. This was more than a little embarrassing. Other vendors had taken notice that I was stuck in the mud. They stared instead of offering to help.

"I guess I should give up, huh, Van?"

He barked.

I glanced in the rearview mirror and caught a glimpse of my reflection. This was not my best moment. My dark bangs stuck to my sweating forehead. Actually, my grandma said we didn't sweat, we glistened. That sounded much more graceful. It didn't help matters that the temperature around the Great Smoky Mountains was hot enough to fry an egg on the hood of my truck.

Late summer had settled around us. An early-morning thunderstorm had dissipated, and the sun was forcing its way out from behind the fading clouds. Unfortunately, the mud hadn't dried up yet. Soon the weather would change, and the green leaves would burst with color. For now, we had to deal with the scorching heat.

My hometown of Gatlinburg was on the other side of the mountains. I was still close enough to home that my overprotective and slightly wacky family could keep tabs on me. I expected to see them pop up at any time. The mountains' peaks blended in with the clouds in the distance. I was now in Cherokee, North Carolina, for the annual Farewell, Summer Arts and Craft Fair.

I'd attended the fair in the past, but only as a patron. It had been almost like a county fair, with rides, games, food trailers selling deep-fried everything, and, of course, the arts and crafts. On the final day of the fair, they held a farewell picnic with hot dogs, hamburgers, and fireworks— sending the summer away with a big bang.

Pounding on the window next to me made me jump. A loud shriek escaped my lips. Caleb Ward stood beside my truck door with a perplexed grimace on his face. His crystal-blue eyes widened. The color reminded me of the hue I used often for the sky in my paintings. His dark hair was in stark contrast to his pale eyes. I lowered the window.

"Need some help?" he asked with a slight hint of Southern drawl.

Now I really was mortified. I hated making mistakes like this. I liked it better when I seemed in control. This was definitely not in control.

"I guess I got stuck in the mud," I said.

"Just a little." He pinched his index finger and thumb together to showcase the amount.

Heat rushed to my cheeks. "This is embarrassing."

"Nothing to be embarrassed about. Good morning, Van." Caleb waved.

Van wagged his tail. Caleb had an adorable German shepherd named Gum Shoe. For that reason, Van had become partial to Caleb. Caleb and I had met recently at another craft fair. Not only was Caleb a talented wood sculptor, but he was also a detective with the Tennessee Bureau of Investigation. Gum Shoe sat near Caleb patiently, waiting for me to get out of this predicament.

I'd rolled up to the craft fair with the best intentions. Selling my paintings was the goal. Plus, having fun with Van and enjoying the beautiful natural surroundings. Scenes like these always helped my muse. The fact that Caleb was here too made it even better. Now if I could only get out of this mess—literally—the day could continue as planned.

"You just need a little traction, that's all," Caleb said.

"How do we do that?" I asked.

"First put the truck in park. Next hand me the floor mat."

I shifted the truck into park and opened the truck door. "Stay put, Van."

After I handed Caleb the floor mat, he said, "Okay, I'm going to put this in front of the tire. When I say go, you drive forward."

"Got it," I said as I slipped back into the truck.

Van was occupied with barking at a cricket that had jumped onto the windshield. I watched in the mirror as Caleb placed the floor mat on the ground.

He stood up and motioned. "Okay, drive forward now."

As I pushed on the gas, the truck and trailer broke free from the mud. I watched through the side mirror in horror as mud splattered all over Caleb's white T-shirt and face. I bit my lip to keep from laughing. The last thing I wanted was for him to see me amused after he'd helped me out of my muddy entanglement. Once I stopped the truck, Caleb walked back to the driver's side window.

I opened the truck's door and got out. "I am so sorry."

Caleb wiped the mud from his face with his hand. "They say mud is good for the complexion, right?"

Mud had made its way into his short hair. I held back the laughter until he let loose. The other vendors watched us as if we were bonkers. Caleb and I continued laughing.

I pulled an old paint rag from my truck and handed it to Caleb. "Thanks again for getting us out."

Caleb swiped the towel across his face. "No problem. Do you need any help setting up?"

I took the dirty towel from his outstretched hand. "Thanks, but I think I'm good."

"I'll see you soon?" Caleb asked.

My stomach danced. "Yes, we're a couple of booths from each other."

"Guess I got lucky with that," he said.

Fortunately, this time Caleb's booth was close to mine. I blushed every time I thought of him. He wouldn't be right next to me, but he would be just a few spaces down. That meant I would see him more often. I hadn't met the people who would be on either side of me, but I hoped they were nice.

I gestured over my shoulder toward the truck. "Okay, I should get to work. See you soon."

Caleb waved as I hopped into the truck and shifted into gear. Van released his high-pitched bark that sounded more like a cricket's chirp.

"Yes, you'll get to play with Gum Shoe later."

Needless to say, the pink paint on my vehicles was now covered with mud. Yes, my trailer was pink and white, and I'd had my old truck painted pink too. Pink was my favorite color, although I loved all colors. Mostly I just wanted everyone to remember me, and standing out with the pink was certainly one way for that to happen. People would never forget my mobile pink art studio. My poor dirty truck and trailer. Now I'd have to wash them soon or everyone would think the color was beige.

I wondered if I hadn't unknowingly selected pink as my signature color because I needed something cheerful. Sometimes the subject matter of my art wasn't so cheery. I'd recently discovered hidden images within my work. Actually, someone else had discovered this by accident when they'd held a glass jar up to a painted canvas. That sounded crazy, but it had actually happened.

Within the paintings were images of skeletons. I had no idea that I'd painted them. The only time I discovered the figures was after the paintings were complete and I held a glass up to my eye for a view. Even though this was a bit spooky, one of the images had helped me solve a recent murder. It could have been a coincidence, but I had a tough time believing that.

I maneuvered my truck and trailer closer to the spot where I'd spend the next week. Most of the area was surrounded by a forest of tall trees. The sun created flickering shadows on the ground as it trickled around the leaves. An area in the middle had lush green grass and would be the spot for the vendors to sell their crafts.

After pulling my trailer up to the location, I shoved the gearshift into PARK. I had wasted almost an hour stuck in the mud, so now my setup time was limited. The craft fair would officially open for the day soon. My fingers were crossed that nothing else would go wrong at the week-long event. There had been enough chaos at the last craft fair. I didn't want that to spill over to this one.

As I got out of the truck with Van in my arms, he whined and squirmed. "Okay, you want to go for a quick walk? We can't be long, though."

The craft fair was being held at a church that had a large area of surrounding acres with the Oconaluftee River running along the edge of the property. They called it a river, but in this area, it appeared more like a creek. My excitement mounted when I thought about spending a week here surrounded by the lush green landscape, Oak, maple, and pine trees stood out against the bright blue late-summer sky. In the early morning before the fair began, I thought it would be great to take my easel down to the water and paint.

Van trotted along beside me as we headed down the meandering dirt path toward the river. Overgrown patches on either side of the trail gave me a creepy feeling that someone was watching us. Water droplets on the leaves from the earlier thunderstorm had almost dried up completely now. Van and I weaved around tall pines as the rays of sunshine trickled through the gaps in the trees. As I stepped over the fallen needles, they crunched under my feet. The pine scent encircled us.

I spotted the river up ahead as the sun sparkled off the water's surface. Gravel in shades of gray and white made up the rocky shoreline. Small waves lapped at the water's edge, with knobby driftwood nearby. Trees hemmed the flow of the water. The only sound came from the creak of the tall trees swaying with the wind, the drone of insects, and the gentle lap of the water against the shore.

"How beautiful, Van," I said.

He barked, his four legs lifting off the ground with the motion.

"What is it, Van?" I asked as he tugged on the leash.

Obviously, he wanted me to see something. He dragged me closer to the water. I caught a glimpse of something on the ground up ahead. It was partially hidden behind one of the trees. As I grew near, I soon realized the legs on the ground were sticking out from behind the tree's trunk. Someone wearing white tennis shoes was there.

"Oh my gosh, Van. Someone's hurt." I scooped him up and rushed toward the person.

As soon as I came upon the woman, I knew she was more than just hurt. She was dead.

CHAPTER 2

*Be aware of your surroundings. You never
know when a customer or a killer might
pop up.*

"We have to get help right away, Van."

I couldn't believe this was happening. I ran away from the body, almost tripping over branches and pine cones as I tried to reach someone for help. Too bad I didn't have my phone with me. I'd left it back at the trailer. I needed to take my phone with me all the time in case something terrible like this happened. But I'd thought we would be alone out there and things would be fine. I was wrong.

Every little noise captured my attention, and I kept glancing over my shoulder as I ran away from the river. It felt as if someone watched me and was chasing me. But I was sure that I was just paranoid because of what I'd discovered. I wasn't sure what had happened to the woman, but it didn't appear to be an accident. I hoped I was wrong.

Just as I came to the end of the path, a tall, dark-haired man popped out in front of me. I screamed. His dark eyes penetrated me. I just knew this was the killer. The woman had been murdered, and this man had done it.

"Are you all right?" the man asked in a creepy voice.

I tried to steady my breathing, but it seemed almost impossible. Why was he asking if I was okay? He probably knew that I'd discovered the woman. Of course, I wasn't okay.

"There's a woman in danger back there by the river. Actually, she's more than in danger. I think she's dead." My voice shook, along with the rest of my body.

The man stared at me. "Is that right?"

"You don't believe me?" I gestured for the man to get out of my way. "Excuse me, but I need to go get help."

It had taken a lot of courage to stand up to that guy. At any second, he could have attacked me too. I moved around him and raced toward the area where the booths were set up. I had to get Caleb right away. As I neared the area, I spotted Caleb. I yelled out to him, and he made eye contact with me. He probably knew by the expression on my face that something was terribly wrong.

Caleb noticed Van in my arms as he ran toward me. "Is everything okay with Van?"

"He's fine. There's a woman by the river. I think she's dead," I said breathlessly,

Caleb stared at me as if what I'd said wasn't computing.

After a few more seconds, he asked, "Can you show me where she is?"

"Follow me," I said.

Caleb and I took off running toward the area. I hoped that it wasn't too late for her, but I was almost positive that it was. We hit the dirt path again, and it felt as if it was an even longer trip to the river this time. Plus, the terrain seemed even rougher. Had more branches been knocked over since the last time I came down the path? They really needed to clear this out. Where had the man that I'd encountered on the path gone? He had acted so strangely that I worried he might be waiting for us.

When Caleb and I came to the river, I pointed to the tree. The woman's legs were still visible from behind the trunk.

"There she is," I said, trying to catch my breath.

I followed Caleb the rest of the way to the tree. We came to a halt when we reached the woman.

Caleb knelt down to check the woman. "She's been dead for a while. Probably at least several hours."

My stunned expression probably said it all, which was good because I was speechless right now. Caleb pulled out his phone and placed a call. I stepped away in the opposite direction. The strange man was nowhere around. Watching the flowing river instead of the dead woman, I listened to Caleb as he talked with the police.

When Caleb got off the phone, he asked, "Do you think you can go back and wait for the police to arrive?"

"Yeah, I can do that," I said.

Actually, I was relieved to get out of there, although I hated leaving Caleb alone.

"Just be careful," he said. "I need to stay here with the body."

"There was one other thing," I said before walking away.

"What's that?" he asked with a frown.

"A man was on the path and popped out in front of me. He confronted me right after I found the body."

Caleb's brow pinched together, and he said, "What did the man say?"

"He asked me if I was all right. I told him about the body I'd found, but he just acted as if I'd told him that I was going for a stroll. It was very strange. After that I took off to find you. I didn't wait for him to say anything else."

"Did you see where he went?" Caleb asked.

"No, I didn't, and I'd never seen him before."

"Okay, just be careful, all right? Text me when you get up there," he said.

"I will," I said, moving away toward the path.

I raced back down the path toward the arts and craft area, hoping the entire time that I didn't run into that man again. After all, he could be the killer. I just knew that the woman's injuries weren't consistent with an accident. Not with the way her neck was twisted.

When I reached the area, I went over to the spot where the police would park. As I stood there, it felt as if someone was staring at me. Glancing to my left, I spotted the man who had been on the path. Frantically, I typed out a text message to Caleb.

That strange man I saw on the path is close by. He is staring at me.

Just stay away from him. We'll have the police speak with him.

Even though I thought the man was creepy, I still wanted to know who he was. So instead of doing what Caleb asked me to do, I walked over to the weird guy. He had been watching me, but when I walked toward him, he acted as if he didn't know I was anywhere around. This guy was strange. Maybe Caleb was right, and I should stay away. The weirdo wouldn't murder me right out here in the open, though, would he?

The man kept his focus in the opposite direction as I approached him. As I neared, I realized he was working on his art project. Instead of looking toward me, he continued putting paint on the canvas in front of him. So he was a painter too, huh? His work was much darker than mine— blackness surrounded fire, monsters, and hideous beasts. It was quite disturbing.

"Excuse me," I said.

"Yes?" His voice dripped with irritation.

"I told you there was a woman injured back there, and you ignored me." I gestured toward the path.

He swiped the paintbrush across the canvas in an angry motion. "What do you want me to do about it?"

"Nothing now. I called for help." I narrowed my eyes. "Are you a vendor here?"

I knew the answer to that by the fact that he

was sitting at one of the booths and had his art-work all around. Nevertheless, I wanted details straight from his mouth.

"Obviously," he said.

Well, he had a sweet demeanor. What a nice guy, I thought, and I meant that in the most sarcastic way possible.

"The police are on their way," I said as a warning to him.

"Good for them," he said, swiping his brush across the canvas.

"I believe someone murdered that woman." I placed my hands on my hips.

A startled expression came over his face. The sirens caught my attention, and I spotted the police cars as they pulled up. I studied his face for a second. He had nothing else to say, so I hurried away to meet the police.

Several police cars pulled up, with lights flashing and sirens blaring. This had captured the attention of quite a few of the vendors. They had no idea what had just happened. Who was the dead woman? Had she been a vendor here too? I was surprised to see Detective Pierce Meyer as he got out of a car. He wore his usual black slacks and button-down shirt with the sleeves rolled up at the forearms.

Pierce had recently become an agent with the FBI. He'd said the change had been in the works for some time, but I wondered if it had anything to do with Caleb. Did he not like working with Caleb? They were competitive, and this only seemed to escalate the more I got to know the two men. Pierce made eye contact with me right

away as he walked toward me. Why had they sent
the FBI?

"Celeste, are you all right?" Pierce asked.

"I'm fine. I'll show you the body. Caleb is staying with the woman until you arrive."

Pierce quirked an eyebrow, but he didn't
comment about Caleb being here at the craft
fair with me. It was a bit strange to have so many
police officers following me. My brothers would
no doubt have made a ton of jokes about this if
they'd seen me. Thank goodness they weren't
around. Though they would be here soon enough.
My entire family would show up for the farewell
picnic at the end of the craft fair. No doubt
something chaotic would occur. It always did
when they were around.

Soon we reached the entrance to the pathway
that led down to the river. Pierce and the officers followed me down the path. The sound of
their steps as they crunched over the dead
branches and pine needles echoed through the
hot air. The water came into view.

I pointed toward the tree. "She's right over
there."

Caleb was nowhere around, and panic took
over. What if the killer had been here and gotten him? Relief washed over me when I saw him
step out from behind the tree.

Officers reached for their guns, but Pierce
said, "Stop. He's a police officer."

Pierce and the other officers moved toward
Caleb. An officer stayed with me, and we waited
back a few steps. Already they had the crime
tape out and were blocking off the area. Pierce

and Caleb spoke with each other while glancing over at me. I knew I had a lot of questions to answer. I checked the time on my phone. I'd miss the opening of the craft fair. Would the coordinators be mad at me for that? Surely, they would understand under the circumstances. A few more seconds passed, and the men walked over to me.

"I'm sorry you had to go through this," Pierce said, touching my arm.

"I was here with her right after, so she felt safe after that," Caleb said.

Pierce frowned at Caleb. Caleb ignored him.

"It was shocking," I said.

"We can go back to your trailer if you'd like. I need to ask you a few questions." Pierce gestured.

"Okay," I said.

Caleb offered me a comforting grin. Or was it his way of saying he didn't want me to leave with Pierce? Reading the men was difficult. Pierce walked beside me as we made our way back to the trailer. Caleb stayed behind to speak with another detective. He'd have to talk to Pierce at some point.

We'd just reached the trailer when a woman approached.

"Is Erica okay? It's her, isn't it? She's the one in danger?" Her voice was full of panic.

I'd seen the grayed-haired woman earlier at a nearby booth when I'd been stuck in the mud.

Pierce directed her to step closer to us. "Ma'am, you're searching for someone?"

"Yes, Erica Miller. She had the booth beside

mine. When she didn't come back last night, I got worried. I thought maybe she decided to spend the night somewhere else. Now, with all the police here, I got worried that something had happened to her."

"Can you describe the woman?" Pierce asked. "What was she wearing when you last saw her?"

"Blue shorts, white shirt, and white tennis shoes. She is such a pretty young girl."

As soon as she gave the description, I knew that the Erica this woman was searching for was the same woman I'd found by the river. I supposed the grimace on my face said it as well.

"Oh no, something happened to Erica," the woman said, staring at me. "Are the rumors true? They found a woman's body by the river? Did she drown?"

"Are you related to her?" Pierce asked.

"No, I just met her last night. She was so nice, though. This is terrible." The woman twisted her wrinkled hands.

"Can you tell me when you saw her last?" Pierce asked.

"It was around seven. Just before dark. She said she was going for a walk. I told her to be careful. I never thought something like this could happen. Did she drown?" the woman asked again.

That means she had to have been murdered sometime between seven p.m. and eight a.m. the next morning. Who would want to strangle her? Was it a random attack by a predator or someone who had it in for Erica? A shiver ran down my spine to think that a killer was out there somewhere. Was it the man I'd discovered on the path? I needed to find out more about him.

I hated to tell the woman that it didn't appear as if Erica had drowned or as if she had been in the water at all.

"We're not sure what happened yet," Pierce said.

"She made the most beautiful metal sculptures. She had a lot of talent. Such a shame," she said.

"What's your name?" Pierce asked.

"Sarah Jane Winchester," the woman said.

Pierce wrote down her name. "We may have more questions for you later."

"Certainly," she said.

"I'm Celeste Cabot," I said, sticking out my hand. "I have the booth here."

She shook my hand. "Nice to meet you, Celeste. I'll be at my booth if you need me."

"Thank you, ma'am," Pierce said.

When the woman walked away, Pierce focused his attention on me again.

"Erica was murdered, wasn't she?" I asked.

The expression on Pierce's face was the answer I had expected. I knew by the injuries that it wasn't an accident.

"We'll know more once the coroner arrives," he said.

Movement caught my attention.

"There's the guy," I said, pointing to the man who had stopped me on the path.

"I'll talk with him. Stay here, and I'll see you before I leave." He touched my arm.

Did he think I was going for another walk? That probably wouldn't happen for a while now that this had occurred. As Pierce walked away, I felt the sensation of being watched. I checked to my left and saw the woman at the booth next to me staring.

When she realized I was watching her, she stepped over to me.

"Good morning. My name is Karla Dean."

"Nice to meet you," I said, stretching my hand out to her.

"I heard what happened. You discovered the body?" she asked.

Word certainly traveled quickly. I briefly explained what had happened.

"That's when I encountered that guy over there," I gestured with a tilt of my head.

Unfortunately, his attention was fixated on us, and he saw me call him out. Plus, he realized that Karla was staring at him too. Pierce was still there, asking him questions, yet the man was glaring at me. I supposed he wasn't happy that I'd sent the police over to talk to him. I couldn't help it, though. He had been near the scene of the crime, and that was something they needed to know.

"I know him," Karla said. "His name is Danny Manslick. I've seen him at other art shows." She rubbed her arms. "He gives me the creeps, and I try to avoid him."

"I get that same vibe. He just popped out in front of me on the path." I scanned the area. "Obviously, it's not as safe as I thought around here."

"I've never heard of anyone not feeling safe here. Though I guess that's all changed now," she said.

"I hope we get some answers soon," I said. "Were you here last night, or did you arrive this morning?"

"I stopped by last night, but I left. I came back this morning," she said.

"Celeste?" Caleb said.

Caleb had walked up to my booth.

"It was nice talking to you, Karla," I said with a wave.

"You too," she said as she eyed Caleb.

After a couple of seconds, she went back to her booth. I was glad to see Caleb. Maybe he had more answers. I still couldn't shake my uneasy feeling. I supposed it would hold on to me for quite some time.

"How are you?" I asked. "Do you have any news for me?"

He ran his hand through his hair. "Nothing definitive yet. I believe she was strangled."

"That's what I thought," I said.

My attention floated over to Danny. At least he wasn't watching me now. Pierce certainly had a lot of questions for him. Maybe they would arrest him soon.

"Do you think that guy did it?" I lowered my voice so Danny wouldn't hear me.

"It's too early to say if that's what happened. We have no evidence yet. I'd say he's a person of interest, though. Of course, this isn't my case," Caleb said,

"I'm surprised they sent the FBI," I said.

"Well, it is federal land. The church only owns the land to that tree line over there." Caleb pointed toward a large oak tree. "The rest including the river is part of the national park."

When I felt someone staring, I checked to the right. Pierce had finished talking with Danny and was headed our way. Caleb peered down at his shoes as if he'd been dreading this time.

"Aren't you arresting him?" I asked when Pierce joined us.

He chuckled. "I don't have reason for that just yet."

"But you admit he is suspicious?" I asked.

"Of course, but that's not reason enough to arrest him," Pierce said.

CHAPTER 3

Mingle with other crafters. Unless, of course, you suspect one might be a murderer. Then maybe you should stay away.

Now that the police had gone, I hoped things would seem less spooky, but so far that wasn't the case. I'd set out my paintings, and the fair had started without a hitch, though word had already spread that there had been a death. Questions were being asked as to why the fair hadn't been canceled. Regardless, I tried to focus on my art, but my mind kept going back to the morning's horrific event.

On the plus side, I'd sold a painting today. It was a landscape of the mountains. There were some paintings I would never sell, though. Not just because they were beautiful to me, but because they had special meanings. I picked up the jar that had held some of my clean brushes and placed it up to my eye. I closed my other eye and peered through the glass at a recent painting of trees and searched for the hidden image.

I found it in the middle. The skeleton was tiny, but he was there. Even though I hadn't added the image of water to the painting, it was there with the skeleton. He knelt down to the river and peered at his reflection. Only the reflection was of the man as he'd been while living. I had no idea what this meant, but I wondered if the river had anything to do with the river here at the fair?

I didn't recognize the man in the image, but now I was more than a little curious about his identity. He had long dark hair and wore a headband around the crown of his hair. Could he be connected to the murder? Should I go to the river now and see if something else came to me? After all, the fair had ended for the day, and I had extra time now. I could take my paints and canvas down by the water.

Yes, I was still creeped out by the thought of being there, but if the images I painted could actually help find the killer, it would be worth it. I'd leave Van in the trailer for a nap. Since the sun would set soon, I knew I only had about an hour to work. Undoubtedly, Caleb and Pierce would think this was a bad idea. That was why I wouldn't tell them.

I gathered up my supplies: a new canvas, paints, brushes, and rags. It was a lot of stuff, but luckily, I had a tote with me to carry everything. After feeding Van, I said good-bye and locked him in the trailer. When I peeked in the window at him, he was already fast asleep. It had been a long day for him, and he was ready for bed. I'd already decided I wouldn't go to the same location where

I'd found the body earlier today. That was too creepy. On the opposite side of the craft area was another path that led to the river. It was a more open space.

With the tote looped over my shoulder, I clutched the easel under one arm and carried the canvas with my other hand. I headed toward the other path. This was also scary since I hadn't been that way since the first day I'd checked out this area. That was the day I'd signed up to be a part of the craft fair.

I wasn't sure what was in store for me, but I'd certainly had no idea what had awaited me this morning either. I hoped there wasn't a repeat this time. If someone else was discovered murdered, I was out of there. No way was I sticking around for a serial killer. One murder was horrendous enough.

I checked over my shoulder several times to make sure no one was following me. I'd kept my eye on Danny all day. Why hadn't the police arrested him? Oh yeah. Not enough evidence. I had my Mace with me, and I was ready to put up a fight. Luckily, when I reached the other path, I saw that it was still much less overgrown, just as I'd remembered it. That gave me a sense of relief. What if I'd walked this way this morning? Would Erica still be undiscovered? The same stillness that I'd experienced this morning surrounded me. Pine trees and oaks shaded my pathway like a canopy, but much more of the sky was visible.

Water flowed along the river, and a warm breeze drifted along my skin. I placed the easel down, trying to make it as steady as possible on the uneven dirt. Next, I propped the canvas up and studied my surroundings. I was all alone. At least I hoped I was all alone. Thank goodness, it wasn't a long walk back to the fair area. I pulled out the paints and brushes from my tote bag to start my work. I figured I'd paint the river and see what happened from there.

As I brushed paint across the canvas, I quickly settled into a zone. It was almost like a trance. Watching the brush stroke across the white emptiness was therapeutic and comforting. It suddenly came to an end, though, when a rustling from over my shoulder caught my attention. I stopped and peered around. My heart sped up.

A squirrel hopped from one branch to another. Whew. It was just a little critter. Van would have loved to chase after that furry guy. My thumping heart settled back to a regular rhythm. I added more colors now, but I couldn't get back in the zone. It felt as if someone was watching me.

I added another image to the painting now. It was no longer just a landscape. The figure of a woman appeared as if painted by unseen hands. Her long, dark hair flowed almost to her waist as she knelt beside the river's edge. She peered into the water as if studying her reflection. I wasn't sure why I'd painted her image, but it was as if she had belonged there in the painting all along. Wait. This reminded me of the hidden image I'd painted earlier. Were the two images connected?

The sound of rustling leaves made me stop. My heart sped up, thumping in my ears loudly. I reprimanded myself for coming down here in the first place. The killer hadn't been caught yet, and I'd thought this was a good idea? Movement came from my right. A woman walked toward me.

She had long black hair that reflected the sunshine like a mirror. She wore a leather dress with beaded trim along the top and the bottom. Moccasins were on her feet, and a band with a feather was around her head.

I didn't know if I should speak to her or run for my life. She didn't seem like a killer, but what did I expect? Someone wearing a Halloween mask and wielding an ax? She certainly didn't have that same creepy glower like Danny.

"My name is Ama," she said in a sweet, soft voice.

For a bit, I was speechless.

After a few seconds, I managed, "I'm Celeste."

She continued walking toward me until she was just a couple of steps away. Instinctively, I backed up a few steps, careful not to fall in the water. She stopped in front of me. Her beauty was even more apparent from up close. Her face was so flawless I could have never painted it with accuracy.

I glanced back at the canvas still on the easel. This was the woman from my painting. Had I seen her somewhere before and unconsciously painted her? How would I explain that I'd added her unknowingly? She studied the image as if she'd read my mind.

"That's me in the painting," she said, pointing at the portrait.

"Yes, I don't know you. Have we met before?" I asked.

"I'm from another time." She surveyed the surroundings.

Her comment seemed calm, as if I should know exactly what she meant. And it clicked. I thought I knew what she was talking about, but I just couldn't believe it. How could this happen again?

"I lived here almost two hundred years ago." She pointed across the river. "My family's land is right there."

A lot of questions ran through my mind. Like why was she here? I thought I already knew how. Well, not exactly how, but I knew that I had painted her here. Call it a psychic ability . . . I wasn't sure, but it happened, and I knew it was all my doing.

"That's a long time. How do you know what year it is now?"

"Since I pop in and out from this dimension to the other, I keep up with things," she said with a wave of her hand.

"Really? Fascinating." I raised an eyebrow. "But why are you here now?" I asked.

"You need me, and I think I need you. Yet I'm not sure how or why."

She sounded just as confused as I felt.

"I don't understand," I said.

"I think when you painted me, I came to this world. I'd been on the other side. The alternate dimension." She pointed into the distance.

"It's not the first time I've done that," I said.

Ama stepped over to the flowing water. She knelt along the riverbank and peered at her reflection, just as she had in the image I'd painted. This was surreal. I expected to wake up. Except I was already awake. I remained still, watching her, and wondering what would happen next.

After a couple of seconds, she faced me. "You connect with the earth for your paintings."

I peered around at the lush trees and green landscape. "Yes, I suppose I do."

Ama walked over to me. "Why are you upset? Something unsettling happened today, didn't it?"

"Yes, something terrible."

"Tell me about the terrible thing," she said.

"Someone was murdered Well, I don't know for sure that she was murdered, but I think she was," I said.

Ama gasped. "Evil is everywhere. It watches us all the time, waiting for the right chance to attack."

Her words rang true for me. It felt as if evil was watching us right now. The sun was setting rapidly, leaving streaks of red and purple across the blue sky, and I knew I had to get back to the trailer soon. There was no way I wanted to stay out here after dark.

"I have to leave now." I pointed toward the path.

"I'll come with you," she said.

I had a feeling she would say that. I couldn't believe I was talking to a ghost. It had happened before when I'd painted a portrait of a woman. She'd appeared in my trailer and had a lot to say. I wondered what Van would think of Ama? He'd liked the last ghost, and I hoped he liked Ama too.

"I suppose you can come if you want," I said.

As if she would listen to anything I said. It wasn't like I could stop her from following me.

I gathered up my things and headed back toward the craft area. Ama walked beside me. She had a bounce in her step as if she was excited about what was to come. Apparently, this was a new adventure for her.

As she kept pace with me, she said, "Do you feel as if someone is watching us now? I think it's more than the trees and the animals."

"The trees watch us?" I asked.

"Of course, they do. They're living things. They know what we're doing." She waved her hand through the air.

Luckily, we were almost at the end of the path. No one had appeared, and I hoped we'd reach the end of the path safely. Ama and I stepped out from the path and into the open grassy area. Lights in the other trailers had been turned on, and some people had set up their tents. I was thankful I wasn't sleeping in a tent. Not with a killer lurking around. It was like some kind of slasher movie. If others were brave enough to do that, good for them, but this girl wasn't doing it.

"My trailer is right over there. I want you to meet someone," I said. "I think you'll like him."

"I like everyone," she said.

We'd just neared the trailer when I screeched to a halt.

Ama stopped beside me. "Is that who you wanted me to meet? I don't like him."

Danny stood near my trailer. He held his arms straight beside him with his fists clenched at his sides. He got weirder by the minute. Without saying a word, he eyed me up and down. Of course, he couldn't see Ama beside me.

"What do you want?" I snapped.

I wouldn't even pretend to be nice to this creep. His eyes narrowed as he glared at me. He didn't appear happy at the way I'd talked to him. I didn't care. He shouldn't lurk around like that and try to scare people.

Without answering, Danny walked away. I suspect he was just trying to intimidate me because I had told the police about him.

"I'm glad he's gone," Ama said.

"Me too," I said.

To be on the safe side, I thought, perhaps I shouldn't go anywhere alone here until the murderer was caught. It was too dangerous. I realized that now after seeing the menacing smirk on Danny's face.

"What are you staring at?" Caleb asked from over my shoulder.

I clutched my chest. "Oh, Caleb, I didn't hear you walk up. Danny was just by my trailer. He gave me this creepy gaze without saying a word. I thought he would be at the police station by now."

"I think they questioned him as long as they could. He threatened to call a lawyer, and they left him alone. There's really no evidence that links him to the crime."

"That's not good to hear." I released a deep breath. "I thought I was safe now."

"I need to have a talk with this guy," Caleb said.

"Who is this?" Ama asked, pointing to Caleb.

Should I tell Caleb about Ama now? No, I should probably wait. One strange experience for the day was enough.

"I'll be back in a bit," Caleb said as he headed down the lane.

"Be careful," I called out.

I wasn't sure if he'd heard me. Of course, I knew he could take care of himself. Nevertheless, I worried.

Ama followed me into my tiny trailer. She peered around in bewilderment. Sure, it was tiny, but for traveling it was plenty of space for Van and me. A sofa changed into a bed and a table. The kitchen area had a cabinet, refrigerator, and cooktop. I'd added pink curtains and cute little pillows to spruce up the space.

"This is your home?" she asked.

"I have a house, but this is my traveling home," I said with a wave of my hand.

Van jumped up and ran over to me. He stopped short when he spotted Ama.

I picked him up and said, "This is Van, my Chihuahua and best friend."

A huge smile spread across her face. "You're beautiful, Van. Such a loving creature."

Van wagged his tail and watched her.

"He likes you," I said.

"I told you he would," Ama said.

I wasn't sure what to say now. I needed to get

dinner and head to bed. I wasn't expecting a guest. Much less one from the spirit world. Ama peered around the trailer again.

"How are you feeling?" I asked. "Did it hurt to travel from one dimension to the other? It seems like it would be a huge energy drain . . . and very tiring."

I yawned just thinking about it.

"I don't feel physical pain," she said. "However, it is sad to be away from my family."

"Do you have a large family?" I asked.

"Yes, I have five brothers, but no sisters."

"I have brothers too. They can be a pain in the rear, but I love them," I said.

"My grandfather's that way. He gets angry with me all the time." Disappointment filled her eyes. "Mostly I try to ignore him."

"I'm sorry to hear that," I said.

Van barked and dashed over to his food dish.

"It's time for his dinner." I gestured.

As if I was watching dissipating fog, Ama was gone. Van and I studied the spot where she'd been standing. Wow, I hadn't been expecting that.

"Where did she go, Van?" I asked, as if he could answer. "Wherever she went, I hope she comes back."

I stepped over to the kitchen area and added food to Van's dish. Once I filled up his water dish, he ran over and wolfed down his late dinner.

Now it was time for me to eat. Though with the stress of the day, I just wanted to go to bed.

I had the painting of Ama propped up against

the wall in my trailer. Stepping in front of it, I studied her face. Her high cheekbones and gorgeous big brown eyes appeared exactly the same in the portrait as when I saw her in ghost form. Retrieving a glass from the counter, I placed it up to my right eye and focused on the painting. I had to know if one of the hidden images would give me an answer about why Ama was here. Maybe one of the images would lead to Erica's killer. I had to admit, that might be wishful thinking.

An image of a skeleton practically popped out at me. I hadn't seen it before. The skeleton was peeking out from behind one of the tall oak trees. The image creeped me out. It was as if the skeleton was watching someone and waiting for the chance to grab the unsuspecting victim. I sensed that this was exactly what the killer had done while waiting to attack Erica. If only I knew the killer's identity. With only the image of the skeleton, that was impossible to know.

CHAPTER 4

Make sure you have all your supplies when you get there. You never know when one of your crafting supplies might need to be used as a weapon in self-defense.

The next morning, I set out my paintings and waited for customers to arrive. The day would be another beautiful one weather-wise, with a bright blue sky and plenty of sunshine. I glanced down the way to see if Danny was anywhere around. In fact, he was sitting outside, working on another one of his creepy paintings. He sent a shiver down my spine.

When an eerie feeling came over me, I scanned the surroundings. Had Ama returned? She was nowhere in sight, but across the way, Sarah Jane was watching me. I tossed my hand up in a wave, but she averted her attention. I supposed she hadn't seen me. Although I thought she'd been staring right at me.

Movement caught my attention. Excitement took over when I spotted a woman headed my way. Thank goodness—I hoped my first customer wasn't my one and only customer of the day. The blond woman wore denim shorts, a white tank, and flip-flops. The frantic expression on her face confused me. Perhaps she just wanted to know where the restrooms were, or the concession stand. The woman walked right up to my booth, but she didn't even bat an eyelash at my paintings.

"May I help you?" I asked.

She peered around as if she was about to reveal a secret. "I need information."

My senses had been correct. She hadn't wanted my paintings at all. I knew she wanted something else.

"The restrooms and concessions are that way." I pointed.

I was surprised that she hadn't noticed the signs when she'd arrived.

"No, that's not what I need," she said.

"Oh, I'm sorry."

I shouldn't have assumed. Now I was just being negative.

"What help do you need?" I tried to sound as pleasant as possible.

"The woman who was murdered. I need to find who did this. I can't wait around for the police to find the killer, so I've decided to check into it myself."

Another amateur sleuth? I hadn't expected that.

"Really?" I asked with a quirked eyebrow.

My attention moved in Danny's direction. He was still working on that horrid painting.

"How did you know the woman?" I asked.

"She was my best friend," the blonde said.

"I'm so sorry for your loss."

I wouldn't tell the woman that I had been the one to find her friend. It would only make her feel worse.

"Thank you," she said in a lowered voice.

"I understand how difficult this is for you," I said.

"Did you see or hear anything that day? Were you here the night when she was murdered?" she asked.

"I didn't come until the next morning," I said, glancing over at Danny.

This time she noticed that my attention was on him. Danny had peered up from his painting too. A darkness flashed in his eyes.

"Who is that man?" she snapped.

I released a deep breath. I hoped she didn't confront him because doing so could be dangerous.

"He's a vendor here. I believe he arrived that night," I said.

"So he saw Erica? Is he the killer?" She had a frantic gaze in her eyes.

"I don't know who the killer is. There's no evidence that he is the killer."

That was the truth and exactly what Caleb or Pierce would tell her if she asked. Maybe I should have kept quiet. Why had I opened my mouth? Oh well. It was already done now, and I'd have to make the best of it.

"I should go talk to him." She walked away.

I rushed over and grabbed her arm. "I don't think that's a good idea."

She narrowed her eyes at me and yanked her arm away. "Why not?"

"He's just a bit odd. The police are talking to him, so you should just let them deal with him."

"I don't think they'll handle it to my satisfaction," she snapped.

Again, me and my big mouth. There was nothing I could do to stop her if she really wanted to speak with him. I needed to calm her down before she did something she would regret.

"Why don't you step over here with me and tell me more about Erica." I gestured to the area outside my trailer.

She eyed me up and down. "All right."

I knew she was still reluctant, but at least this was a step in the right direction. She directed her attention to Danny as she walked with me closer to my trailer.

"You were friends with Erica?" I asked when we stopped.

"Yes," she said in an agitated tone. "I already told you that."

"My name is Celeste Cabot," I said, sticking out my hand for a shake.

She eyed me up and down as if she might suspect me of having had something to do with her friend's fate. She didn't shake my hand either. "April Beaumont."

"Nice to meet you, April. I wish we were meeting under better circumstances," I said. "I'm sure that the police will find who did this soon."

She scoffed. "How can you be so sure? Do you know them or something?"

"As a matter of fact, yes."

Nothing I said was making her feel better. "Well, tell them to hurry up. I have a lot of questions for the vendors here. I know someone here knows something. Did they see anything that night? It's extremely important that I find this out."

I knew she was upset, but her questions were a bit odd. She seemed panicked as if this was urgent. Of course, it *was* urgent, but she hadn't given the police a chance to find the killer yet.

"When was the last time you saw Erica?" I asked.

She fidgeted when I asked that question. "Um, I saw her earlier in the day before she was killed."

"Did you work together?" I asked.

She fidgeted her hands again. "I work at Cherokee Bakery. Erica worked at the elementary school. She was an art teacher there."

I wasn't sure what other questions to ask, but I wanted to find out more about their friendship.

"I need to go now. I can't answer more questions." She walked away.

She headed back down the path and away from the festival grounds. At least she wasn't going to confront Danny. However, he had disappeared. Every time I didn't have my eyes on him, he seemed to do this. I wondered where he'd gone.

That was certainly a strange encounter. I needed

to find out more information about April. At least, I had her name and knew where she worked.

I went back to my painting, hoping that a customer would arrive. After a few minutes, I sensed someone watching me again. Over the top of his canvas, Danny peeked out at me. That was way too creepy for my liking. He creeped around, and I never knew when he would pop up. I should just walk up to him and tell him to knock it off. Instead, not budging, I placed my hands on my hips. He didn't even bother to stop staring but just kept watching me for what seemed like an eternity. After a few seconds, his gaze moved back to his canvas.

I wasn't sure how much more I could handle of him. Had Pierce or Caleb found any additional information that they would share with me? They'd probably be surprised that I had info for them.

Movement out of the corner of my eye caught my attention. Scanning my surroundings, I noticed Ama standing over by the side of the trailer. As she motioned for me to come over to her, she peeked around the corner of the trailer as if hiding from someone. I didn't see anyone that she might be dodging. As far as I knew, I was the only one who could see her.

I walked over to her. "Ama, you're back. I thought you weren't coming back. Are you hiding from someone?"

"I didn't want the others to see me," she said.

"Do you think they can see you?" I asked.

I assumed I was the only one who could see

her, but maybe I was wrong. That assumption was based purely on past experience.

"I don't know," she said.

"I don't think they can see you," I said.

"Are you certain? I don't want to cause any harm for you."

"I don't think anyone would be upset even if they saw you. They would think we were friends."

"Friends? I like that," she said around a giggle.

Maybe Ama needed a friend. I was still cautious, though, because I didn't know much about her or why she was here. My family constantly reminded me to be suspicious of everyone. I knew they were just trying to help, but we were surely a guarded bunch.

"You should test it out. Walk up to someone else and talk to them. If they respond, you know they see you."

She shook her head. "Oh no, I couldn't do that."

"Why not? You came up to me and talked." I pointed at the booth across from me. "I think that woman is nice. Just act as if you are interested in her merchandise. There's no harm in that."

She stared across the way for several seconds and said, "I suppose there's no harm in that. Okay, I'll do it."

"Would you like me to walk with you?" I asked.

She shook her head. "No, I want to see if I alone will attract her attention."

I watched as Ama walked across the path toward the booth. She approached the woman, and so far, the vendor hadn't noticed Ama, though she was working on one of her silver and white beaded jewelry pieces. I'd spotted those earlier when I'd walked by her booth.

Just as Ama stepped up, the woman focused right on Ama. Wow, so maybe she could see Ama. The woman raised her arm and waved. She was staring in my direction. Oh no. She had noticed me watching. I waved back. The woman went back to her jewelry. So she hadn't seen Ama after all. Maybe that would make Ama feel better.

After a few more seconds, Ama came back. "You were right, Celeste. She didn't notice me at all. I don't know whether to be happy about that or sad."

Now I felt bad for her.

"Well, I think if people open their minds to the possibility, they'll be able to see you. Or if you have something important to tell them, they will be able to see and hear you."

"Do you think I have something important to tell you?" She eyed me expectantly with her big brown eyes.

That was a question I was asking myself.

"I'm not sure, Ama. Maybe you'll remember."

Ama shook her head. "Maybe I will, or maybe I won't. I think there is one place that will help me remember."

"Where's that?" I asked.

Please don't let her say the river. I knew it was a mistake going back the last time. It's true that

I had met Ama that way, but would that turn out to be a bad thing too?

"I want you to go back to the river with me. It calls to me and tells me to bring you there," she said.

As tempting as that sounded, I knew I would have to pass. The river calling to me made me uneasy. Had it called to Erica too? Ama could be luring me there so someone could murder me. I hated that the thought crossed my mind, but I could never be too careful. After all, I didn't know her.

"I can't do that," I said.

"Why not?"

"Someone was murdered by the river. It isn't safe."

The scowl remained on her face. "But I met you there."

"That was a mistake on my part. I don't think I should go back."

"You have to do more painting there. That will help you find answers."

"How do you know this?" I asked.

"The spirits tell me this."

What spirits? There were more spirits at the river? One was enough. She seemed sincere, though.

"I'll think about it. I can't go right now anyway. I have customers."

She peered around, and of course, no one was approaching my booth.

"Well, I anticipate customers soon. It's still early."

Thank goodness, a customer actually approached. The woman had saved me and didn't even realize it. Though, as soon as she was gone, I would have to answer Ama again. I'd told her I'd think about going back, and that was the truth. I was torn between how sincere she seemed and how guarded I felt I should be. After all, the painting I'd done at the river had brought her to me. Plus, it had the hidden image. Maybe I could paint another hidden image, though I didn't see why I couldn't attempt it from the safety of my little trailer.

I explained the inspiration for some of my paintings to the customers as Ama watched. She was probably waiting for her chance to ask me again.

After a couple of seconds, though, I checked for Ama. She had disappeared again. It was just as well because I felt I needed time to think. Maybe she was gone for good this time.

CHAPTER 5

Signs are important. Not only those that tell customers about your products and prices, but other kinds of signs. Watch out for warning signs, like that a killer is lurking.

Ultimately, the woman bought a landscape painting from me. I was pleased by this, and it motived me to pull out a new canvas and start another landscape. After buying a batch of lemon bars from a vendor a few booths down, I'd devoured one of the delicious treats and now sat in front of my booth. Van sat in his bed beside my feet, watching the people as they strolled around the festival. His one ear perked up, and I knew he was on alert.

"What's wrong, Van?" I asked.

When he did this, it always made me wonder what was about to happen. Usually, it just meant a squirrel was nearby or someone wanted to step up and check out my art. He'd grown used to the strangers coming by, though, and now I felt he enjoyed them. When I caught movement out of the corner of my eye, I knew why he'd had his ear perked up so much. Caleb and Gum Shoe were headed our way.

A smile spread across Caleb's face as soon as he realized I was watching him. Van barked in excitement at the prospect of playing with Gum Shoe. Mostly he just liked to cuddle up to the bigger dog, and the German shepherd tolerated it. I put my brush in the jar beside me and wiped my hands on an old rag. I picked up Van and stepped over to the edge of the trailer to meet Caleb and his dog.

"How are you doing?" Caleb asked with concern in his voice.

"I'm okay. Any news?" I asked with anticipation.

"Nothing new," he said.

A deep breath slipped out when I'd meant to hold in any signs of my disappointment. "That's discouraging."

"Unfortunately, it comes with the business." Caleb's attention focused on Danny's booth. "Is he still acting weird?"

"Yes, but I don't think it's an act. He definitely is weird."

"We're keeping an eye on him," Caleb said.

"So he's your number-one suspect?" I asked.

"As of right now, yes, he is a suspect. There certainly isn't much to go on, though," he said. "I came by earlier, and I thought you were talking with someone. It was odd, though, that I didn't see anyone around. Gum Shoe wanted to go in the opposite direction, so I didn't come over to talk."

Oh no. He must have seen me speaking with Ama. I had hoped to keep that a secret. Caleb knew I'd seen another ghost, but now I had to tell him there was a new one? I wasn't sure that was a great idea.

"I was probably talking to Van," I said.

"That's what I figured," he said.

Though I wasn't sure I believed him.

"How's the painting going?" Caleb asked. "Any new mysterious things showing up?"

My hesitation probably told him the answer. I debated whether I should confess the current situation. Caleb had been more understanding than I'd imagined he'd be, so I decided to tell him exactly what was happening.

"Yes, there has been a development," I said.

"Another ghost?"

I nodded. "Yes, another ghost."

It felt good to get that out there.

"Is the ghost here now?" Caleb scanned the surroundings.

"Currently, no. She tends to pop in and out."

"Apparently ghosts like to do that," he said.

"There must be some kind of supernatural portal," I said.

"Who is she?" he asked.

I surveyed the area to see if she had shown up again. There was no sign of her. "Her name is Ama. I was painting down by the river, and she just appeared."

"You were painting by the river? When?"

Oh no. Now I had to tell him about that mistake.

"Yes, I went back to the river. It was not at the

same spot where the body was found. That would have been creepy. In my defense, it was as if the river was calling to me. I realize that it was a mistake," I said.

"Celeste, that is too dangerous. The killer is still out there. He could be waiting for his next victim."

Movement caught my attention. I spotted April Beaumont again. Why had she returned? She had been watching us from a distance.

"Or she," I said.

Caleb followed my focus and glanced in April's direction.

"Do you know her?" I asked. "She came by to talk with me."

"That's the best friend, right?" Caleb asked.

"That's what she said when she came by here not long ago. She was asking questions. I guess she doesn't feel the police are doing enough to find the killer."

"She hasn't been ruled out as a suspect," Caleb said.

My eyes widened. "Really? Why do you say that?"

"I can't tell you any of that just yet," he said.

Now I'd have to find out on my own. They should just tell me these things and save me time.

April moved around the side of a trailer and disappeared from view. I had a feeling it wouldn't be the last that I saw of her.

"There's a great café in town, and I wondered if you'd like to go there for dinner later? They have the best burgers in the world." Caleb flashed his gorgeous white teeth.

I knew instantly that he was referring to my aunt's café. Ever since I'd taken him there, he'd been obsessed with her hamburgers. I had to admit they were the best I'd ever had, and I wasn't biased. Well, maybe a little.

"Sure, I'd love that," I said.

"Great. So I'll meet you here at eight?"

Van barked.

"He says eight is fine."

Gum Shoe chimed in with his bark too.

"I guess we're all set," Caleb said. "I'll see you later."

I watched as Caleb walked back down the path toward his booth. Now I had to find a way to speak with April again. Why would she be considered a suspect in the death of her best friend? Especially since she'd been here and asked about possible killers. She was trying to find her friend's murderer. That seemed like what a best friend would do. Though I supposed the police had their reasons.

Things had died down, and the festival was over for the day. I still had an hour before my dinner date with Caleb. That still gave me time to do some snooping around. Since seeing April and then Caleb saying that she was a suspect, I couldn't get it out of my head. I wanted to go by her work and speak with her again. I had no idea if she'd be there, but I had to check it out nonetheless.

Van and I climbed into my pink pickup and

headed toward the bakery. I'd been there before, but I tried to avoid the temptation of their decadent cupcakes. I wasn't sure if I'd be able to visit today without a purchase. Luckily, they stayed open late. That was because not only did they sell baked goods, but they had sandwiches and such too.

I rolled up to the bakery and found a parking spot along the street. It hit me. They wouldn't allow Van inside. I'd already arrived now, and there wasn't time to take him back to the trailer. There was no way I was leaving him in the truck.

Movement caught my attention. Out of the corner of my eye, I saw my grandmother waving her arms at me.

"Well, what do you know? Grammy's here, Van," I said as I scooped him up.

Craft Fair Lemon Bars

Crust
   2 sticks unsalted butter
   1 cup all-purpose flour
   ½ cup granulated sugar
   ¼ teaspoon vanilla extract

Filling
   6 eggs
   3 cups granulated sugar
   1 cup all-purpose flour
   1 cup lemon juice

1. Preheat oven to 350 degrees F. Grease a 9- x 13-inch baking dish.

2. Place 1 cup flour and butter in a mixing bowl. Combine thoroughly. Add ½ cup sugar and vanilla extract. Mix together until crumbly like cookie dough.

3. With moistened fingers, press dough into bottom of baking dish.

4. Bake crust on center rack for 20 minutes or until lightly golden brown.

5. Beat eggs in a bowl. Whisk in sugar and flour until smooth. Add lemon juice.

6. Pour lemon custard over crust.

7. Bake at 350 degrees for twenty minutes until filling is set.

8. Let the pan cool and then place in refrigerator for a couple hours until chilled.

9. Dust with powdered sugar.

CHAPTER 6

*Have a checklist so you don't forget anything.
This goes for murder clues as well as art
supplies.*

Van barked, and his tailed wagged quickly, like a tiny propeller. We got out of the truck and walked over to meet my grandmother. Her large white Cadillac was parked a few spots down from me.

"Grammy, what are you doing here at this hour?" I asked after giving her a hug.

"Darling, Grammy still drives, you know. Plus, I'm allowed out after four p.m. I don't have a curfew yet." She rubbed Van's little apple-shaped head.

Sadly, I knew all too well that she drove. However, I didn't like the idea of her tooling around after dark. She insisted she was fine with driving and nothing had changed since her sixteenth birthday. That was sixty-nine years ago. A few things had changed, but I wouldn't argue that fact.

"Which store did you go to?" I asked.

She showed her bag. "I went to the hardware store for some nails."

"Why do you need nails?"

"I'm rescreening my porch."

My eyes widened. "Grammy, you can't do that."

"Why can't I do that? Is it against the law?"

"You'll hurt yourself."

Van barked as if he was agreeing with me.

"Whose side are you on, Van?" She placed her hand on her slender hip. "I am perfectly capable of fixing the porch."

"If you wait until later, I'll come over and help you."

She waved her hand. "Oh no, you're busy and don't have time for me."

Now she was making me feel guilty.

"Of course, I have time for you, Grammy."

"Well, we'll see," she said.

That was her way of saying she was going to do it anyway. I'd have to hurry up with dinner and get over to her house before she did anything.

"Where are you headed, dear?" she asked.

I was surprised she hadn't mentioned the body that had been discovered down by the river. She knew I was at the craft fair this week. At least, I'd told her I would be there. I was sure the murder would be the talk of the town. Not to mention that I'd been the one to find Erica.

"Grammy, have you seen the news?"

I wished I could keep it from her, but I knew she'd find out soon enough. The last thing I wanted was to upset her.

"I've been busy," she said.

Doing what? What other home-improvement project had she tackled?

"There was a murder at the festival," I said matter-of-factly.

Her eyes widened. "Why haven't I heard about this?"

"I don't know, but I promise things are fine, so you don't have to worry."

"Not worrying? That won't happen," she said. "This is terrifying. Do they know who did this?"

I grimaced. My facial expression gave her the answer.

Her hand flew to her mouth. "The killer is still out there? Oh, Celeste. You need to leave that festival right away."

"I need the money, Grammy."

"I can give you some money." She unsnapped the clasp on her pocketbook.

I stopped her. "No, Grammy. I need to make my own money. It's important for my self-esteem. Plus, I can make money to buy you a pretty birthday gift."

"Oh no. Don't you give me a thing," she said.

"We'll see," I said.

She knew what that meant since she'd used that line on me.

"The police are on the scene, and they'll probably find the killer soon," I said, trying to sound reassuring.

"You're not going to try to find the killer yourself, are you?"

I gestured over my shoulder back at the bakery. "I thought it wouldn't hurt if I helped research some of the clues."

She shook her head. "I love you, Celeste, but I don't agree with the things you do sometimes."

Ignoring her comment, I said, "I need to ask a favor, Grammy."

"What's that, dear?"

"Can you watch Van for just a few minutes while I go into the bakery?"

I wouldn't tell her that the bakery was part of my clue research.

"Sure, we'll sit right here on this bench. Come to Grammy, Van." My grandmother took Van from my arms and headed toward the bench positioned on the sidewalk.

"I'll be back in just a few," I said from over my shoulder.

I hoped something came of this visit. Opening the bakery door, I stepped inside and was greeted by the scent of vanilla and spice. The bell above the door chimed, announcing my arrival. No one was behind the counter, and there were no customers either. I stood in the middle of the room, unsure what to do next.

"Hello?" I called out.

After a few seconds, a gray-haired woman peeked out from around the swinging door that led from what I assumed was the kitchen area.

"Sorry about that." She stepped out from behind the door and over to the counter. "I was just cleaning up."

Yes, it was about closing time, and I didn't want to take up too much of her time.

"It's no problem," I said.

"May I help you?" she asked as she wiped her hands on her apron.

I couldn't just ask questions without making a purchase. The sacrifices I made in the name of investigating. I peered into the display case. There wasn't much left. Muffins, cookies, and a few cupcakes.

"I'll have a red velvet cupcake, and a chocolate one." I pointed.

Grammy loved red velvet. She deserved a thank-you treat for watching Van.

"Coming right up," the woman said.

Now was my chance to ask questions.

"Is April Beaumont working?" I asked, peering back toward the kitchen area.

"She's already gone for the day, but she'll be working tomorrow." She placed the cupcakes in a couple of boxes. "Are you friends with her?"

"We just recently met."

"I suppose you know what happened." The woman's expression turned bleak. "I told her to take a few days off. In light of what happened, she needs to take some time."

"That's probably a good idea," I said.

"And to think they were arguing before she was killed—that's such a tragedy. Now that will be the last memory April has of Erica. They loved each other, but everyone fights sometimes." She placed the boxes on top of the counter and gave me my total.

"Yes, they do," I said, handing her my credit card.

April and Erica had argued? I couldn't believe what she'd said. Maybe that was why Caleb said the police considered her a suspect.

"Do you know why they were arguing?" I asked, trying not to sound too eager for the answer.

She handed me the credit card back. I signed the receipt, still waiting for a response.

"It was silly . . . ," she said with a nervous chuckle. "I'm sure it wasn't true."

She was torturing me by dragging this out. Now I *had* to know the reason behind their spat.

The woman scanned the room as if someone would overhear her. As far as I knew, we were the only ones in the bakery.

"April thought Erica was going out with her boyfriend," she said in a lowered voice.

My eyes widened. "That's certainly a reason for an argument. Was he cheating with Erica?"

"Not that I know of, but I suppose I don't know them that well. Just what April told me and what I overheard."

"Why did she accuse Erica of that?" I asked.

Could this have been a love triangle gone horribly wrong? I wanted to ask for April's boyfriend's name, but this woman might assume that I should know. Did Pierce or Caleb know this information?

"I suppose Erica and Mark had been together," she said. "As in they were hanging out as friends."

At least now I had a first name. How would I get his last name?

"I didn't know Mark well. What's his last name again?" I asked.

"Patterson," she said without hesitation.

Finding this information had been easier than

I'd expected. Wouldn't Caleb and Pierce be impressed with my detective skills? Okay, probably not. Nevertheless, I was proud of how easily I'd found the details.

"And he works here at the bakery?" I asked.

"Oh no. I don't think he does anything other than the photography. He's not too good at it either." She lowered her voice. "I think he works out of his home. He's not that busy, if you know what I mean."

I nodded. "Yes, I guess I was confused about where he worked. Thank you for the cupcakes."

I wanted to thank her for the information, but she had no idea that she'd helped me.

"Should I tell April that you stopped by?" she asked.

That was the last thing I wanted.

"I'll give her a call. Thank you," I said as I headed for the door with the cupcakes in hand.

Grandma was still sitting on the bench with Van on her lap. He was enjoying watching the people and traffic.

"I got you a thank-you gift." I handed her the pink box. "It's red velvet, your favorite."

Van sniffed the box.

"You didn't have to do that," she said.

I knew she was happy that I had, though.

"Did you find out anything?" She gestured toward the bakery.

Nothing got by grandma. She'd known the reason for my visit.

"Actually, yes, I discovered some interesting information." I picked up Van.

"I just hope you're careful." She opened the box's lid and sniffed the cupcake. "What if you find the killer and he knows you know? He could come after you."

"I won't let that happen," I said.

The thought did scare me a bit. I walked with my grandmother over to her car.

She opened her car door and slipped behind the wheel. "Just be careful. If you need backup, call me."

"I will," I said around a laugh.

"I'm serious."

I stopped my laughter. "Absolutely, I will call you."

"I'll see you soon?" she asked.

"As soon as possible," I said.

"I refuse to wait until Christmas to see you," she said.

I shook my head. "It won't be that long."

She cranked the engine. "It had better not be that long."

With Van in my arms, I stood on the sidewalk, watching my grandmother drive away.

"Well, Van, I guess we're finished here. Now what should my next move be?" I rubbed behind his ears.

When I spun around to go to my truck, I was startled to see Pierce there. He didn't seem that surprised to see me, though.

"How are you?" Pierce asked as he approached.

"Fancy seeing you here," I said with a nervous laugh.

He motioned toward the bakery. How had he

known where I'd been? I remembered the cupcake box in my hand. Oh yeah, that was a dead giveaway.

"I just got a cupcake," I said.

Now I even sounded guilty.

He leaned against the truck and crossed his arms in front of his chest. "What else did you discover while you were in there?"

"What do you mean?"

"I just thought it was odd that you came to this bakery."

"I like the cupcakes," I said.

"You come here often?"

"I'm watching my calories," I said.

"Right. It's just a coincidence that the murder victim's best friend works here."

I raised an eyebrow. "Oh, does she? I had no idea."

"I appreciate the help with the investigation, but we have everything under control."

Well, I wouldn't argue with him, but I thought otherwise.

Pierce studied my face. "What about dinner tonight?"

I didn't want to tell him that I already had plans with Caleb. When I didn't answer right away, he knew something was wrong.

"You already have plans, don't you," he said. "That's okay, I understand."

Apparently, my face had given it away. Wasn't he going to ask if I was available for another night?

"Just be careful, Celeste. Let us handle the investigation," he said.

"I'm always careful," I said.

"I'm sure I'll see you at the fair," he said.

"Thank you for the invitation. And yes, I'll be at the fair," I said.

I didn't know what to say, so I said nothing else. He walked away. Now I felt even worse. What else could I do? After checking the time on my phone, I realized I only had a few minutes until it was time to meet Caleb. I hurried into the truck with Van and headed back toward the fair.

I enjoyed Caleb's company, but now I would be preoccupied by the information I'd learned at the bakery. Finding April's boyfriend would have to wait until tomorrow. Maybe I could do some checking around early in the morning before the fair. If I had to wait until later in the evening, it would feel like an eternity. Soon I had reached the fair area again. I pulled the truck back up to the spot behind my trailer.

"Van, you have to stay here and take a nap while I go out with Caleb. Gum Shoe will keep you company."

I knew Caleb would bring Gum Shoe over to visit with Van. They'd probably just nap, though. We climbed out of the truck just as Caleb was walking up.

"I guess I have good timing," he said.

"We took a quick trip," I said.

He noticed the cupcake box in my hand. I hoped he didn't put two and two together.

"I'll just put this away. Gum Shoe can come in with Van," I said.

Thank goodness, Caleb didn't mention the cupcake box. Though that didn't mean he wouldn't ask about it later. After putting the dogs in the trailer, I walked over and climbed into Caleb's truck with him.

Soon Caleb and I arrived at Patty's Paradise Café in Gatlinburg, just on the other side of the mountains. My aunt had the best food in all of Tennessee. Actually, she made the best food ever, but maybe I was a bit partial. Caleb had been obsessed since I'd brought him here for our first date. The burgers were almost like magic. Aunt Patty never revealed her secret, although I'd asked many times.

Caleb parked up front, and we hopped out of his truck. For a split second, Pierce's face flashed through my mind. He'd seemed upset when he'd found out I already had dinner plans. What could I do, though? Maybe I should ask him for ice cream. What would Caleb say if I brought him to Aunt Patty's too?

Caleb held the door open for me, and I stepped inside. "Thank you."

"You're welcome," he said.

The smell of the burgers and fries hit me. Aunt Patty was behind the counter and spotted us right away.

She tossed her hand up in a wave. "Celeste and Caleb. Just the two people I wanted to see."

Uh oh. Was there a problem? She never said that. We stepped over to the counter. Anxiety settled in my stomach.

"Is everything all right, Aunt Patty?" I asked.

"You tell me," she said as she wiped her hands

on a towel. "What is happening over at the fair? I called your mother, and she told me about the murder. Said you're okay, but we're both worried."

I released a deep breath. "Is that all?"

"Is that all?" Caleb and Patty said in unison.

"Wow, there's an echo in here," I said.

"There's no reason to worry, Patty. I'm taking care of her."

I held my hand up. "I am fine."

"That's probably what that poor girl thought before the killer found her," Aunt Patty said with a wave of the spatula.

This was certainly putting a gloomy mood over our dinner.

"Don't worry, Aunt Patty. Things will be fine," I said.

"I certainly hope so. Now you all go sit down, and I'll get your orders on the grill. I assume you want the usual."

"Yes, the usual, I suppose," I said.

Caleb and I had only been here a couple of times together. How many visits had Caleb made alone since I'd brought him here? He most likely was truly addicted now. Caleb and I went over to the booth where we'd had our first meal together.

"You can understand why your aunt is worried about you, can't you?" Caleb said.

"Yes, I can understand, but we can't let being cautious stop us from proceeding with the fair. Do you have any clues?" I asked as I slid across the booth's bench.

He studied my face. "It doesn't seem good, Celeste. Though we do have a footprint. It's a large size, so we're thinking it's a man."

Aunt Patty brought over our drinks.

"Thank you, Aunt Patty," I said.

"Yes, thanks, Patty," Caleb said.

"You're welcome, sweetie. I'll be back in a jiffy with the food." She winked at Caleb.

When she left, I picked up the conversation again.

"A fresh footprint? I suppose if anyone other than the killer had been back there, they would have discovered the body, just like I did."

He sipped on his water. "I think so, yes."

"Interesting," I said, taking a drink of my Diet Coke.

"Don't tell anyone I gave you this information," Caleb said.

"I won't say a word." I pretended to zip my mouth.

"You're not going to check everyone's shoes now, are you?" Caleb asked.

"Of course not," I said with a wave of my hand.

Yes, I had planned on checking everyone's shoes. At least Danny's. He was the prime suspect, as far as I was concerned.

"What size shoes do you think they were?" I had to know this to continue my investigation.

"Size thirteen," he said.

How would I know for sure Danny's shoe size? It wasn't like I could come right out and ask him. Having this detail was better than nothing, though. And could I rule out Danny if his shoe size didn't fit?

"We should change the subject." Caleb took a bite of his burger.

Caleb insisted on discussing other things as we finished dinner and topped it off with large servings of Aunt Patty's chocolate cherry cake. After finishing our food, we paid Aunt Patty and headed outside. She never wanted to accept money from Caleb, but she never had a problem taking it from me. I would have insisted she take the money anyway. Everyone in my family tried to pay for each other's stuff. It was an ongoing battle. Aunt Patty thought Caleb was a cutie.

Darkness had settled around us as we'd enjoyed dinner. I couldn't help but be a bit nervous about this. After all, there was a killer out there somewhere.

Aunt Patty's Chocolate Cherry Cake

1 (18-ounce) package chocolate fudge cake
   mix
21 ounces of cherry pie filling
1 teaspoon almond extract
2 eggs
1 cup white sugar
5 tablespoons of butter
⅓ cup milk
1 cup semisweet chocolate chips
Whipped topping
Cherries
Chocolate candies

1. Preheat oven to 350 degrees F. Grease a 9- x 13-inch baking dish.

2. In a large bowl, combine cake mix, cherry pie filling, almond extract, and 2 eggs. Stir until well blended.

3. Pour batter into the greased pan. Bake at 350 degrees for 30 minutes.

4. Combine sugar, butter, and milk in a small saucepan. Bring to a boil and stir constantly for 2 minutes. Remove from heat and stir in chocolate chips until smooth.

5. Pour over the cake and garnish with whipped topping, cherries, and chocolate candy.

CHAPTER 7

*Have business cards. Potential customers
might not buy now, but later, they'll have your
information to call. Make sure not to let the
ghost knock your cards onto the ground,
though, because then your Chihuahua might
chew them up.*

At five a.m., I was startled awake by the sound
of footsteps. I shot up in bed. Van barked, so I
knew he'd heard it too. It hadn't been a dream.

"What was that, Van?" I whispered.

Unfortunately, Van couldn't answer. I picked
him up from the bed as I climbed out. I hurried
over to the little window and peered outside. It
was still dark, so it was hard to see if anyone was
out there. I couldn't say for sure what the sound
had been. With a murderer on the loose somewhere out there, though, it was unsettling.

Nothing seemed out of place, and a few people had already set up their wares. No one seemed
panicked, so I figured the noise had just been
one of the normal sounds associated with a fair.

I decided to get my day under way too. Waking up early would give me extra time to search into the few leads I had for the murder. Like finding out Danny's shoe size. I placed Van down and headed for his food and water dishes. I'd only taken a couple of steps when I came to a screeching halt. Ama was standing in the tiny kitchen area of my trailer. She grinned when she realized I'd spotted her. Had she been the one to make the noise that woke me?

"Good morning!" She waved.

"I wasn't sure if you were coming back," I said.

"I'm still here to help you," she said.

If by "help," she meant wanting me to go down to the river again, that was totally out of the question. I didn't want to seem rude, but I wasn't sure what she was here to help me with. My paintings? Finding the killer?

"I appreciate your help, Ama," I said.

"As soon as day breaks, we'll go back to the river?" she asked with hope in her voice.

Oh no. Now I had to tell her no again.

"Ama, I just don't think it's safe for me to go there." I put food in Van's dish and filled the other with water.

"The killer wouldn't go back there again. Aren't there people watching the area?"

I wasn't so sure about that.

"Besides, I will protect you," she said.

As sweet as that offer was, I didn't feel a ghost could offer much protection from a killer.

"I don't think it's as easy as that," I said.

Van raced to his dish and chomped on the food.

"I feel strongly that you should go back to the river and use the energy for your paintings." She watched me with her big brown eyes.

As I contemplated what she'd said, I straightened up in the kitchen, putting the few dishes I had back into the cabinet from the night before. I supposed that since I had painted Ama's image while at the river, maybe the energy there was good for my paintings. Plus, I needed another clue to point me in the direction of the killer. Maybe one of the hidden images would provide that.

"I'm sorry, Ama, but I can't go right now. I have other things to check out. There's someone I need to see," I said as I grabbed a protein bar.

Unfortunately, living in a trailer and having limited time meant I couldn't always eat a warm breakfast.

"Can I go with you?" She batted her dark eyelashes at me.

"Well, I suppose that would be okay," I said, taking a bite from the bar.

After putting a black T-shirt on Van that read STUD MUFFIN across the back, I dressed in a white T-shirt and jeans and hurried out the door. I stopped in my tracks when I spotted Danny outside his trailer.

"Whoa. There's the bad guy," Ama said.

"Yep. That's him. I need to find out what size shoe he wears," I said out of the corner of my mouth so that no one would see me talking.

"How will you do that?" she asked.

"That's a good question. I have no idea."

"Where's he going?" Ama leaned closer to me.

"I just hope he stays away from me," I said.

Danny walked away from his trailer in the opposite direction. That meant he probably wouldn't be gone long. If I wanted to find his shoe size, I would have to act quickly. My heart pounded, and my knees shook, but I forced myself to move forward.

"Are you going inside his trailer?" Ama trailed along behind me.

"I suppose I have to if I want to find his shoe size."

"What if he only has one pair?"

"I'll be in big trouble."

When I neared his trailer, though, I couldn't believe my luck. A pair of flip-flops sat beside the door.

"I can't believe my luck!"

"Hurry, before he sees you," Ama urged.

I rushed over and grabbed the dingy yellow flip-flop.

"What size is it?" Ama asked excitedly.

My eyes widened. "Size thirteen!"

Ama's hand flew to her mouth.

"Exactly what I thought," I said.

"Hey, what are you doing?" Danny yelled.

He sprinted toward me. I tossed the shoe on the ground and ran for my life. Speaking of life, mine flashed before my eyes. I had to make it to my truck and escape. My breathing was labored as I pushed my legs to move as fast as possible. Thank goodness, my truck came into view. I wasn't sure if Danny was still following me, but checking would only slow me down. Once I reached the truck, I jumped inside and shoved the key into the ignition. Danny wasn't there.

"Whew. That was a close one," I said as I cranked the engine.

"I'm glad he didn't get you. He'd probably snap you like a twig." Ama sat on the passenger side of the truck's seat.

I placed Van in his car seat between us. "Sadly, though, I realize that just because Danny has the same shoe size as the police found at the scene doesn't mean he was the killer. I still need more proof."

"At least you tried. Now what will we do?" Ama asked.

I'd gotten lucky and through an online search found April's boyfriend's address.

"We're on to the next mission," I said as I stopped at the red light.

"What kind of mission is this?" Ama asked.

"I tracked down April's boyfriend, and now I want to speak with him."

"Are you sure this is a good idea?"

"Absolutely," I said as I pushed on the gas.

Van barked as if he agreed with me.

As I navigated the streets, my apprehension increased. I hoped this guy wasn't mean and would actually speak with me. What if he called the police? I was about to find out. However, when I pulled up to the apartment, he was leaving. Where was he going? This would mess up my chance to speak with him.

I parked toward the back of the lot to see what he did next. Mark got in his car and backed out.

"I suppose if I want to speak with him, I will have to see where he goes," I said.

"Who is this man?" Ama asked.

"Someone I want to speak with about the murder," I said as I pulled out and fell in behind his car.

It was kind of hard to go undercover while driving a pink truck, though, thank goodness, Mark had no idea who I was and wouldn't be suspicious.

I navigated the streets, keeping up with the red Toyota. Even if he didn't know me, he might wonder why a pink truck was following his every move. He pulled up in front of the Java Hut and parked the car. I managed to pull along the curb a few cars back. He sat there without getting out of the car. Was he wondering what I was up to?

After a few more seconds, he got out of the car and headed toward the coffee shop. What if this wasn't even Mark? It hadn't hit me until now that I could have followed the wrong person. After all, I'd never seen him before. Maybe this was his roommate. There was only one way for me to find out for sure. I'd have to speak with him.

"I guess we're getting coffee," I said as I unbuckled my seat belt.

"Sounds like fun to me," Ama said in a peppy tone.

We got out of the truck. I wasn't sure if they'd allow Van inside the coffee shop. I hoped so because otherwise I'd have to wait outside for the man. We headed down the sidewalk. Well, as far as the strangers thought, it was just me and my dog walking down the sidewalk. No one seemed to notice Ama. In fact, a man had walked right through her. He didn't miss a step as he continued down the sidewalk, though he did act as if he'd sensed something.

"Did you feel that?" I asked.

"Not a thing," Ama said.

When I reached the coffee shop, I saw the sign in the window: NO PETS. Now what? I peered over at the guy's car. Would he notice if I checked inside his car? Perhaps I could spot something with his name on it. He'd probably think I was stealing something. I had to think of a way to get closer so that I could see in the windows without appearing suspicious. That seemed virtually impossible. I placed Van down on the sidewalk and held his leash.

"Don't you have to go potty, Van?" I asked.

Luckily, Van walked over to the landscaped area. There was a tree that was near a bench. The landscaping decorated the street all along the main section. He sniffed around a bit, and I used that as an excuse to incher closer to the parked car.

I peered over my shoulder toward the coffee shop to see if the man was on his way out. It was hard to see inside the windows, but it appeared as if he was still at the counter. Would he come outside to sit, or would he get his order to go? I leaned closer to the car and peered inside.

"Do you see anything interesting?" Ama asked as she stood on the sidewalk behind me.

"His car sure is messy. There could be stuff in there, and I wouldn't even know it because of all the trash inside," I said as I cupped my hands around my eyes to get a better view.

Just as I was about to give up on spotting anything important in the car, I saw the photos. Maybe my eyes were deceiving me, but I thought for sure the photos were of Erica. Why were there so many of them? And they weren't all photos that had been posed for either. Some of them seemed as if he'd been watching her from afar and snapped the shots. That was assuming he was the photographer. Since the woman at the bakery said that was what Mark did for a living, it would make sense that he'd taken the photos.

I made sure that he hadn't exited the coffee shop. The last thing I needed was this guy to catch me peeking into his car if he was the killer. Now what would I do? Should I speak with him still? Or should I tell Caleb or Pierce about what I'd seen. Just the photos in his car didn't prove anything. Nevertheless, it was creepy. I should hang around and see what he did next, though I couldn't just stand here by his car. Van and Ama patiently waited for me to make my next move.

"We'll sit down at one of the tables outside the shop," I said as I picked up Van.

People would just think I was talking to Van and not Ama too, since obviously they couldn't see her. Once at a table, I watched inside the coffee shop. The guy I thought was Mark was paying for his purchase. I still couldn't tell if he was planning on sitting inside, coming outside to sit, or just getting an order to go. What would I do if he sat down? Start a conversation? That would be awkward. Even more of a problem would be if he decided to leave. Would I follow him to the next stop he made?

Mark took his coffee and bag from the barista. My heart sped up as he walked toward the door. I would have to make a decision soon. When he stepped out from the coffee shop, his attention fell right on me. I was like a deer caught in the headlights. He quirked an eyebrow but averted his gaze.

Apparently, he thought I was strange. Thank goodness, he didn't move toward the car, though. Moving to the right, he sat down at the table across from mine. Now I was really faced with a dilemma.

"Are you going to speak with him?" Ama asked.

I couldn't answer her because Mark might hear me. He'd think I was even weirder. He probably wondered why I was sitting there without coffee. If he asked me, Van would be my reason. How would I start a conversation with this man? He was reading on his phone while I sat there awkwardly fidgeting, as if waiting for someone to arrive. Starting a conversation wasn't so tough, but segueing into the recent murder would be hard.

Ama sat in the chair beside me. "Aren't you going to talk to him?"

I grimaced.

"You'd better say something before he leaves," she said.

I supposed Mark felt me watching him because he caught me in the act. Now he probably thought I was flirting with him. The thought made me want to get up from the chair and leave right away. Nevertheless, I remained seated and vowed to see this through, no matter how tough it got.

"I'm waiting for someone," I said.

He nodded as if he thought I was an annoying gnat. If I'd been sitting close, he probably would have swatted at me. He didn't seem very nice, but maybe I'd caught him at a bad time. Though if he was the killer, that would certainly explain his attitude.

"You have to keep this up," Ama said. "Really go at him."

It was surprising to see her act so spunky when initially she'd been so shy. I liked that she was being more comfortable with me now.

"Do you like the coffee here?" I asked.

He stopped staring at his phone long enough to answer. "It's okay."

I was at a loss for what to say next. Without saying a word, he got up from the chair. Oh no. Was he leaving? I'd chased him away before I'd had a chance to ask any questions.

"You have to stop him from leaving," Ama said with urgency in her voice.

I knew that all too well, but I had no idea what to do to keep him there. I couldn't jump out in front of him and block him from getting into his car. He would call the police. Or maybe he'd want to get rid of me like he had done with Erica. That thought sent a shiver down my spine. He didn't head toward his car, though. Instead, he was headed straight for my table. Panic rushed through me. I'd wanted to speak with him, but now I was having second thoughts.

"Oh no, what is he doing? He's headed this way," Ama said.

I stopped myself from screaming. It was difficult to breath now.

"Do you mind if I sit down?" He gestured toward the chair across from me.

What? He wanted to sit with me. Uh oh. Maybe he had thought I was flirting after all. His expression still wasn't exactly friendly, but it was an improvement from his earlier demeanor.

"Sure, that's fine," I said.

This was so awkward. I supposed it would be easier to speak with him, but I still didn't know how I would bring up the subject of murder.

He sat down at the table across from me. "Are you drinking coffee?"

"I'm waiting for a friend so that she can go inside and order for us." I pointed to Van. "Dogs aren't allowed inside."

He didn't speak to Van. That wasn't very nice.

"So you're not waiting on a boyfriend?" he asked.

"I think you have to let him woo you," Ama said.

Woo me? I might be hyperventilating

"No, I'm not waiting on a boyfriend," I said.

When the words came out, it sounded as if I might be sick or had cotton in my mouth.

"What's your name?" he asked and took a drink of coffee.

"Celeste," I mumbled.

"You need to sound a bit more enthusiastic than that," Ama said. "He won't want to woo you."

I should hope not.

"I'm Mark," he said.

"Did he wiggle his eyebrows?" Ama asked.

Was I supposed to be impressed that I was in his presence? Van growled at Mark. I felt the same way as Van. Mark acknowledged Van with a frown. Surely, he sensed that I wasn't interested.

"You're very pretty. I hope you don't mind if I tell you that," Mark said.

It kind of gave me the creeps, actually.

"Listen, I'm a photographer, and I would love to take your picture sometime. I can tell that you'd be photogenic."

I bet he'd used that line a thousand times. I'd probably heard it almost that often. He should come up with something new and original.

"I'm kind of camera shy," I said.

He scowled as if this was the worst thing I could have said. I needed to get on to the subject of the recent murder. That was the whole reason for this encounter.

"Actually, I think I've seen you before," I said.

The line between his brow furrowed. "Really?"

"Yes, I'm sure I've seen you before. Are you April Beaumont's boyfriend?"

His eyes widened as if he couldn't believe I'd mentioned his girlfriend's name. Believe it, buddy.

"Yes, she is my girlfriend," he stammered. "Well, we were kind of dating."

"I don't like him," Ama said.

Van barked. We all saw through his act.

"I heard what happened to her friend. That's horrible. Do they have any idea who did that?"

I had taken enough time talking to this guy, and I wanted to get straight to the point.

He knocked over his coffee cup, spilling the light brown liquid across the table.

"Not that I'm aware of," he said, picking up the cup.

"I guess it was tough since you'd been arguing with April about dating Erica."

I took a chance and mentioned this. I had no idea how he would react. He didn't respond, as if he'd lost the ability to speak.

"Were you actually dating Erica?"

Maybe he really was, and that might explain the photos. Though they were still creepy and stalkerish.

"Who are you again?" he asked with a frown. "I don't remember April mentioning you."

"Well, we were friends. How else would I know about your fight?"

He studied my face.

"I'm sure April doesn't share everything about her life with you," I said.

He narrowed his eyes as if the thought of this made him angry. I sensed this guy had a temper. I didn't want to see the full force of it either.

He leaned back in the chair. "Yes, Erica and I were dating."

Wow. So he was admitting it. I wondered if he had admitted this to April. He had to wonder whether, if I was friends with April, I would tell her now. I felt as if I needed to tell her if she didn't already know. How would I share this news with her, though?

Anxiety coursed through my veins. This definitely made him a suspect. Perhaps I was in over my head here. What would I ask him next? It wasn't as if I could just come out and ask him if he'd murdered Erica. Well, I supposed I could, but killers typically didn't confess. Sometimes they did, though. They liked to brag about what they'd done. I was so confused.

"When was the last time you saw Erica?" I asked.

This sounded more like questioning from the police. I hoped he didn't get suspicious.

He eyed me again. "The afternoon before she was murdered."

I couldn't believe he'd actually answered me.

"What was she doing? What was her mood?" I pressed.

He scowled. "Why are you so interested in what she was doing?"

I knew it wouldn't be long before he became suspicious of my questioning.

I kept my cool. "I guess you can imagine that women are afraid for their safety. Is there a serial killer on the loose?"

"Oh, yeah, I guess that would upset you. A serial killer? Is that what you think happened?" he asked.

He almost seemed amused, and it seemed as if there was a bit of a grin trying to creep through his expression. Maybe my imagination was running wild, though. At least, I'd given him a satisfactory answer. Now maybe he would continue answering my questions. Caleb and Pierce would definitely disapprove of what I was doing.

"It's a possibility until the police discover what happened to Erica. What do you think happened?" I placed the ball back in his court.

"A random serial killer is probably what happened," he said.

Was he just saying that because it was the answer I'd given him?

"What did she say the last time you talked with her? You know, maybe she mentioned having an encounter with someone? A fight?"

"Are you insinuating that April did this?"

He was defensive of April now. Maybe he knew more than he was letting on about their fight.

"I didn't mean that, but they were arguing over something you did. That has to make you feel bad."

After I said that, I wished I could take it back. This would only make him mad.

"April would never do anything like that," he said.

He pushed to his feet. I supposed this meant our conversation was over. For now. I wouldn't give up on finding more information from him, though. After all that he'd admitted, I felt this could be the lead I was waiting for to find the killer. He tossed his cup in the trash and headed for his car without saying another word.

"Well, at least he didn't litter," Ama said.

Yes, at least there was that. Mark got into his car, cranked the engine, and sped away from the curb as I still sat there contemplating all that had happened. Where had I gone wrong with my questioning? Was there something else that I could have asked or done to make this go better? Probably so. After all, I was just an amateur at this. My specialty was painting.

"I suppose we should go now," I said, reaching down for Van.

He barked in agreement. After I picked him up, we headed down the sidewalk toward my truck. Ama walked along beside us.

CHAPTER 8

*Be available to answer customers' questions.
Ghosts can be distracting, but you have to put
your foot down and let them know that the
customer comes first.*

We were back in the truck now. I sat there for a bit, wondering what to do next. Should I quit for the morning or pursue this just a bit more?

"What are you thinking, Celeste?" Ama asked.

"I think I shouldn't give up on this lead. It seemed so strange the way he acted, and I think he knows much more about this than he's telling me."

"Do you think he killed Erica?" Ama asked.

"It's a possibility."

She rubbed her arms as if fighting off a cold chill. "It's scary just thinking about you talking with him. What if he wanted to hurt you?"

"It's a risk I had to take. The pictures he had of Erica in his car were disturbing. Why did he have so many? Was he obsessed with her?"

"An obsession that turned deadly." Ama's words hung in the air.

It was exactly what I'd been thinking. How would I prove it?

I pulled out my phone. "I'm going to do a bit more research on him."

"It's lucky you have that device to help," Ama said.

I scrolled through his Facebook page, hoping for something interesting. I noticed that he wasn't friends with Erica. She had a page, but they weren't friends. Had he been friends with her? Once April found out about their affair, had she made him get rid of her? I spotted one man who seemed to comment on Mark's posts the most. They seemed to be good friends. Perhaps I could speak with him about Mark and find out more. The man's name was Russell Anderson, and he worked at the local photography store. I supposed they shared an interest in photography.

I pulled up to the photography store and put the truck in PARK. "Well, here we are. I suppose I should go in and see if he'll speak with me."

"It can't hurt, right?" Ama asked.

"I certainly hope not," I said.

I got out of the truck with Van in my arms and Ama beside me. I hoped the store's staff didn't make me leave because of Van. He wouldn't harm anything, but I totally understood why they would have a no-pets policy. We stepped inside the store. There were no customers, but I supposed that was because it was so early. A couple of men were working behind the counter.

"Welcome to Photography World," the dark-haired man said.

I recognized him from the picture on his Facebook page. It was Russell.

He made eye contact with me and came over.

"May I help you?" he asked.

I had no idea about cameras, so I wouldn't even pretend that was why I was there. What if he told Mark I had been asking about him? It was definitely risky speaking with Mark's friends. How would I explain my questions? Anxiety gnawed away at me. Russell eyed me expectantly.

"Are you okay, Celeste?" Ama waved her hand in front of my face. "Are you frozen?"

I snapped out of it and asked, "I'm investigating someone you know."

Apprehension filled my voice, even though I tried to sound confident. If I was going to track down a killer, I needed to build up my self-confidence. No one would want to talk with someone who sounded scared all the time.

His eyes widened. "Who?"

"Mark Patterson," I said. "You know him, right?"

"Oh, Mark. I knew you were going to say him. Yes, I know him. We're not that good of friends."

It seemed like Russell was already trying to distance himself from Mark. Was that because he knew he was guilty of something?

"I need to ask you some questions about Mark. Is that okay?"

What would I do if he said no? I shouldn't have given him the easy way out. I should have acted as if I would insist on having my questions answered.

"Yeah, I guess it's okay. What do you want to know about him?" Russell asked.

"Was he dating Erica Miller?" I asked.

His expression turned solemn. "I heard what happened to her. It's terrible. I hope they find out who did it."

"That's why I'm trying to learn more about her," I said.

"Are you with the police?" he asked.

"Something like that," I said.

He raised an eyebrow. "I don't think they were dating. He's been with April for a while now."

"That's what I thought, but he told me he was seeing Erica. That they were having an affair," I said.

He scoffed. "If they were dating, she never let on about it."

"Did you know Erica too?" I asked.

"We've spoken on occasion, but I didn't know her well. We went to the same gym."

He didn't act as if he knew anyone well.

"What did you talk about?" I pressed.

"We'd say hello and stuff. I remember this one time she expressed her displeasure with Mark following her."

My eyes widened. "He followed her?"

"That's what she told me. I believe her too. That's what makes me think he isn't telling the truth. Maybe he wanted to date Erica."

"Do you think Mark was following her all the time?" I asked.

"Yes, I think so," he said.

"What makes you think that?"

"Just from what she said, I guess. I even saw him lurking outside the gym. When I asked him about following her, he said he was meeting Erica there. As if she wanted him to meet her." Russell picked up a camera and fiddled with it.

If Erica and Mark really were dating, it would be understandable that he would meet her at the gym. Maybe Erica hadn't told the truth? But why would she lie about something like that? To keep the fact that she was cheating with Mark from her friend April?

"This doesn't sound good," Ama said.

"You really can't trust anything this guy says. I don't see what April sees in him. She should have dumped him a long time ago. He lies a lot," Russell said.

"So he tells a lot of lies?" I asked. "Why are you friends with him?"

"I guess I feel sorry for him because he doesn't have a lot of friends. Besides, they're all just tall tales, so I figure what's the harm in listening to the stories he makes up."

It could be dangerous if it got someone killed.

"Did he say anything to you about what happened to Erica?"

"I mentioned it, and he completely ignored my comment."

"That is odd."

He'd said Mark was an odd person, so I shouldn't be too surprised.

"Do you think he had anything to do with her death?" I asked.

"I'd like to think not, but I guess anything is possible."

The door opened and a couple of customers walked in. One headed toward the digital section, and the other, a woman, approached the counter. The other employee stepped around to help the man across the room.

"Sorry, but I have to go." Russell gestured toward the woman with a tilt of his head.

"Sure, I understand. Thanks again for talking with me."

"You didn't need camera equipment?" he asked with a confused frown as if he'd just realized I'd never asked for photography assistance.

"No, I'm good. Thanks again." I hurried out of the shop before he had a chance to ask more questions.

I hopped back into the truck with Van.

Ama sat beside me again. "This is confusing. Why would Mark lie about dating Erica?"

"That's a good question. I don't know if we'll ever figure out the answer," I said as I made a left.

In the rearview mirror, I caught a glimpse of a black car behind me. The car stayed with me. Normally, that wouldn't capture my attention, but this car seemed like it had been making every move I made. Plus, I thought I remembered seeing it at the camera store. Was this person following me? Soon we arrived back at the festival.

I parked the truck behind the trailer and hurried to set out my paintings. I was late, and the directors of the festival wouldn't be happy if they saw that I didn't have my paintings out yet. In my defense, they hadn't warned me that there would be a murder to investigate. I rushed around setting everything up, while Ama and Van watched.

"Good work," Ama said.

"Thank you," I said as I blew the bangs out of my eyes.

An odd sensation fell over me. Soon I realized that my neighbor had been stealthily spying on me from behind one of her canvases. I realized that she must have noticed me talking to Ama.

I chuckled, trying to brush off what she'd seen. "I was talking to my dog."

Van was fast asleep in his little bed. Ugh. The woman quirked an eyebrow.

"I didn't realize he'd fallen asleep and wasn't listening."

She still had a raised eyebrow. Whatever. I didn't care what she thought of me. I had business to attend to anyway. After a few seconds, she went back to her business. I'd have to be more careful in the future. It was hard to remember that I wasn't talking to a living person that everyone saw too. Ama seemed so real to me.

Only a couple of minutes had passed when I felt someone watching me again. From my left, I spotted Danny staring at me. That sent a shiver down my spine. What did he want? He was creepy, and his mannerisms were more than a little unsettling. I frowned at him, hoping that he would take a hint. Only he didn't seem fazed. His eyes pierced right through me. I wasn't sure what to do next.

"Why is he staring at you?" Ama asked.

"I don't know," I said out of the corner of my mouth.

I would just act as if I hadn't noticed his strange behavior, though it was hard to ignore. It wasn't like I could go up and ask him. Who was this guy anyway? Did he have friends and family? What would they tell me about him?

As I finished up a painting, I noticed movement out of the corner of my eye. Pierce was speaking with Danny. I wished I could overhear the conversation. I watched for a couple of minutes, but nothing about their body language gave me a clue about what they were saying. Danny kept his same uninterested demeanor. Pierce pointed at Danny in what I assumed was a warning. What was that all about?

When Pierce stepped away from Danny, I spotted Caleb headed toward Danny's trailer. Caleb and Pierce eyed each other as Caleb approached, as if they had just stepped into the boxing ring and were sizing each other up before the match. The stare-down lasted a few seconds until Caleb headed over to speak with Danny.

Pierce stood there watching the men talk. It felt as if I needed to step in and stop whatever was going on between the two men. I picked up Van and headed over toward Pierce. He had no idea I was walking up behind him because he was too fixated on Caleb and Danny.

"What's going on between you two?" I asked once I was standing next to Pierce.

After a couple of seconds, he blinked and

snapped out of his trance. "Celeste, I didn't know you were standing there."

"Obviously," I said. "You were really focused on what they're doing. What's happening with you guys?"

"Nothing. Why do you ask?" He tried to act causal.

He knew what I meant.

"I thought you might throw a few punches," I said.

"No, it isn't like that."

I knew they were competitive, but they had ramped it up lately.

Touching Pierce's arm, I said, "Why don't you come over to my trailer and have a glass of lemonade?"

He seemed reluctant at first, but he said, "Lemonade sounds good."

We'd shared a glass of lemonade before while sitting in front of my tiny trailer. That had been at night under the stars. Now was a completely different scenario. Pierce walked toward my trailer with me, but he peered over his shoulder at Caleb several times on the way. I hoped he didn't sneak back over when I went inside for the lemonade. Caleb was so busy speaking with Danny that he wasn't even paying attention to Pierce or me.

When we reached the trailer, I said, "I'll be right back with the lemonade. Why don't you hold Van?"

Van had a way of calming people down. How could anyone be upset when seeing his sweet face? Pierce took Van in his arms. Van already had a soothing effect on Pierce. I stepped inside and grabbed a couple of plastic cups from the cabinet. My mother and grandmother had taught me to always have a cold beverage ready for unannounced guests. The pale-yellow liquid trickled down over the ice cubes. Too bad I didn't have fresh lemons to garnish the side of the cup. I picked up the lemonades and headed back outside. Pierce was still standing there with Van in his arms.

I handed him the cold glass of lemonade. "I can put Van to bed. He's probably sleepy."

"Are you sure? I don't mind holding him."

Van was snuggled up next to Pierce's neck.

"Well, I suppose if he wants to stay . . ."

Van would snuggle next to anyone if they'd let him.

I pointed toward the folding chairs. "Why don't you have a seat?"

He paused but sat down. I took a seat in the chair next to him. We drank in silence.

I asked, "What's the deal with you and Caleb?"

"What do you mean?" he asked.

"I think you know what I mean. I saw the way you all were glaring at each other."

He took another drink. "I don't know what you mean."

Obviously, he wasn't going to tell me anything. Caleb had stepped away from Danny now, without even a glance in our direction.

"What did you find out about Danny?" I asked.

Van was sitting on Pierce's lap now.

"We've asked him to come in for a polygraph test. At first, he said he would do it, and now h` says no. That we'll have to talk to his lawyer."

"That doesn't sound good. It seems as if he's trying to hide something."

"That's what I think," Pierce said. "We have no way to force him to do it, though. There's not enough evidence to arrest him."

I wondered if I should tell Pierce about what I'd learned from Mark Patterson. Yes, it was probably the responsible thing to do. I wanted the killer behind bars.

"Have you spoken with someone named Mark Patterson?" I asked.

"April's boyfriend?" Pierce asked.

"So you have talked with him," I said.

"He doesn't seem to have any information."

"He said he was having an affair with Erica. That would make him a person of interest and make you want to question him, right?" I asked.

"He said that?" Piece seemed surprised by this revelation.

"That's what he told me. The woman at the bakery told me that too. Though I spoke with a friend of his named Russell, and he said he didn't believe Mark. He said that Mark makes up a lot of stuff."

"Well, you've certainly been busy with this investigation," he said.

I hoped he wasn't mad about that.

"Just trying to get to the bottom of things," I said.

"Celeste, this could be dangerous. I really don't think you should be involved."

I knew he would say that. Maybe it was time for me to change the subject.

"How do you like your new job?" I asked.

I often wondered if the reason he left the local force was because of Caleb.

"I'm enjoying it," he said. "Sometimes it's nice to have a change. Plus, I've always wanted this opportunity."

He finished off the last of the lemonade.

"Would you like more?" I asked.

"I really need to get back to work. Thank you for being so nice to me," he said.

His blue eyes would make anyone melt.

"Just being nice to someone," I said.

"Would you like to go to dinner one night when you're not too busy?" he asked.

"Me too busy? I'd think it was more about when you're not too busy," I said.

"Well, I always have to make time for dinner." He flashed a lopsided grin.

"I've seen you eating sandwiches while standing up and doing your work. You don't even take time to sit down."

"I suppose I have been busy lately," he said. "So what about that dinner?"

"The festival will be over soon," I said.

My answer was vague. I hadn't said yes, but I hadn't said no either. Of course, I'd done that on purpose.

He pushed to his feet and handed Van back to me. "I really should get going. Please, Celeste, let us do the investigating."

I forced a grin. "Sure thing."

I knew I wouldn't stick with that. After all, I hadn't promised. I was on to something, and I didn't want to give up now. Our fingers touched, lingering for just a bit as Pierce handed the cup back to me. My heart sped up with our interaction. After a couple of seconds, Pierce broke away, and my trance stopped. He rubbed Van's head one last time and headed away from my trailer. I watched until he moved around the corner.

CHAPTER 9

Be kind, even if you're greeted with a bit of unfriendliness. If there's a murderer on the loose, you'll need all the friends you can get.

Later that evening, I decided I would take a stroll down the path just a bit. Not too far, because I was always scared that the killer might show up. My trailer was still in sight, and I knew exactly where I was headed. Van walked on his leash beside me. To anyone watching, it appeared that I was just taking my adorable little dog for a walk. That was true. However, I was planning something else as well.

I was walking past Danny's trailer. I wasn't sure what I hoped to accomplish by this, but I wanted to feel as if I was doing something to solve this crime. Not trying wasn't an option. Crickets chirped in the nearby trees, and the stars sparkled in the night sky. A hint of the cool fall air that would arrive next month carried across the wind. Within seconds, it had disappeared, and the warmth settled around us again.

A light appeared in the tiny window of Danny's trailer. I assumed he was inside. The thought sent a shiver down my spine. Just thinking of his creepy face gave me the chills. What was he doing in there? Plotting his next murder? What I didn't understand was what would have been his motive for killing Erica? He had to have one, right? I had no idea what I would do if he came out of his trailer and saw me. I'd probably run.

Maybe if I could just take a peek in the window. However, that was an invasion of privacy, and I certainly wouldn't want anyone to do that to me. That was why I kept my blinds down at night. This was an emergency, though. I could be saving someone's life if I found out Danny was the killer. I scanned the area to see if anyone was watching me.

The few people who remained outside seemed to be finalizing their items for the evening. I eased over to the trailer with adrenaline coursing through my veins. Standing on my tiptoes, I inched up to the window.

Just as I peered inside, I heard, "*Psst, psst.*"

Van barked, and I moved away from the window. When I spun around, I spotted Caleb standing by the edge of Danny's trailer. I hurried over to him. He pulled me behind the trailer and indicated for me to be quiet by placing his index finger up to his mouth. My heart thumped in my chest. I hoped that Van wouldn't bark and reveal our hiding spot. Surely Danny would hear Van and would come out to inspect.

As the trailer door squeaked open, I held my

breath. Caleb motioned for us to move farther back from the trailer. I tried to be quiet, but my feet crunched a large twig on the ground. It snapped, echoing across the night air. Danny had to have heard that sound.

"Let's get out of here," Caleb said.

Caleb grabbed my hand, and we ran away from the trailer. The area was open until we reached either the church or the wooded space behind the church. Danny could still see us if he happened to check behind his trailer. Catching us running would let him know that we were up to something suspicious.

After what seemed like running a marathon, Caleb and I ran around the side of the church and stopped so that we could catch our breath. I leaned my back against the brick building. We remained silent as we tried to recover from our exertion; the only sound was our breathing. Van had been quiet as he went along for the adventure. I held him in my arms, and he sniffed the air as if this was just another stroll around the festival.

"Do you think he saw us?" I asked after a few more seconds.

"I don't think he came back there to check things out before we got away. At least I didn't see him," Caleb said.

"That was a close one," I said.

"Celeste, what were you doing?" Caleb asked.

I knew he'd ask that. "I was just walking."

"I know that's not the truth. You were walking and snooping around someone's trailer. You've talked me into spying in people's trailers before. You have to stop doing that."

"How else can I see if they're up to no good?" I asked.

He shook his head. "You don't see what I'm saying at all. Just let us investigate."

Pierce and Caleb were on repeat with that saying. They should try something else.

Silence settled between us again.

After a few seconds, Caleb asked, "Did you see anything?"

I knew he'd want to know. My snooping around wasn't so bad, after all. "I didn't have time before you caught me," I said.

"What did you expect to find?" Caleb asked.

I wouldn't admit that I had found Danny's shoe size. Caleb would surely think I'd lost my mind. Maybe I had lost it. Even if the size was the same, it still wouldn't prove that Danny was the killer.

"I thought maybe he would be writing a confession letter," I said.

Caleb remained silent. I supposed he didn't share my sense of humor over the matter.

"Seriously, Caleb, I'm just trying to help. This involves me too. I have to worry about my safety."

"That's exactly why you shouldn't be snooping around," he said.

"There are better ways to find the killer."

I screeched and jumped. Ama was leaning with her back against the church, just like me. Caleb jumped and thrust his hands out in a defensive stance.

"What happened? Did something bite you?" Caleb eyed me up and down.

I supposed I had to tell him that the ghost had said something. Ama needed to stop popping up like that.

"The ghost said there are better ways to find the killer," I said.

I might as well just come out and say it.

"What ghost?" Caleb asked as he scanned the area.

I gestured beside me with a flick of my wrist.

"There's a ghost beside you?" Caleb whispered. "Where did she come from?"

"I met her down by the river. She lived on this land."

"How many years ago?" Caleb asked.

"Many," I said.

"Interesting," he said, staring at the empty space beside me. "Do you know why she's here?"

"She said she's here to help me," I said.

"Help with what?" Caleb asked.

"Finding the killer, I suppose," Ama answered.

"Her name is Ama, by the way. She thinks she can help find the killer."

"Oh no. Another amateur sleuth? I don't know if I can handle another one," Caleb said.

"I'm only trying to help," I said.

"Celeste, I appreciate the help. I don't want you to think that I don't." Caleb wrapped his hand around mine. "It's just your safety, you know?"

My hand tingled from his touch.

"Put your hands up," the male voice boomed from somewhere to our right.

Caleb let go of my hand. He stuck his arms in the air. I placed one arm up, while holding Van with my other. Ama placed her hands in the air as if the man could see her. On my right, I spotted Pierce, with his gun pointed at us.

"What are you doing?" Caleb demanded.

Pierce lowered the gun and put it back in the holster. He walked over to us. Caleb lowered his arms, but I wasn't quite sure yet. I was still shocked by what had happened.

"What are you all doing out here?" Pierce moved his attention from me to Caleb. "You can put your hands down, Celeste. I'm not going to shoot you."

"Celeste was snooping around Danny's trailer. I caught her peeking in his window," Caleb said.

I couldn't believe he'd told on me.

"I wasn't guilty yet. You caught me before I had a chance to do it," I said.

Pierce shook his head. "I'd barely gotten away from here when I got a call about two suspicious people hiding behind the church. You can imagine I thought it might be the killer."

"Sorry about that," I said.

"If you were snooping around Danny's trailer, how did you end up hiding behind the church?" Pierce lifted an eyebrow.

I had to admit I seemed guilty.

"When Danny came out of the trailer, I didn't want him to see us lurking around, so we ran away," Caleb said.

"That doesn't sound professional," Pierce said.

Now I was causing more friction between them.

"I did what was necessary," Caleb said defensively. "I'll walk her back to her trailer."

"I can walk her back," Pierce said.

"That won't be necessary. I got it." Caleb motioned for us to start walking.

"I can walk myself back," I said.

"It's too dangerous," they said in unison.

"Okay, how about you both walk me back."

I had to do something before they fought right there by the church. They scrutinized each other with their eyes. When they didn't answer, I simply walked anyway. Soon they'd fallen in step beside me. This was completely awkward, being escorted back to my trailer with two cops on each side. At least I felt safe. I hoped they didn't argue once I was back in my trailer.

Silence settled between us as we walked across the open space toward the trailers. I wondered who had called the police on us. Had it been Danny? I wondered if he'd seen Caleb and me after all. It was possible that he knew he was calling the police on us and not a couple of random people. Soon we arrived back at my trailer. I paused at the door, facing Caleb and Pierce.

"Good night, men. No more competition tonight," I said.

Pierce and Caleb raised their eyebrows as if it was a synchronized move. They knew what I meant.

CHAPTER 10

Smile and greet customers, even if you're terrified. You don't want to look like you've seen a ghost—even if you have seen one.

As soon as I set foot in my trailer, I noticed the paper on the floor. Was it something that I'd dropped? I reached down and picked it up. Anxiety slowly trickled in as I unfolded the paper. Maybe someone had left me a note.

I know what you're doing.

I released an audible gasp. My stomach churned, and my heart sped up. What did this mean? Who had left the note? I opened the trailer door and peered out to see if Caleb and Pierce were still around. They'd already gone. Should I call them and let them know about this? I hated to ask them to come back here after they'd just left. I was causing yet another problem for them. I should just wait until the morning.

What if the killer had left the note and came

back for me? I slammed the trailer door shut and quickly locked it. I placed the note on the counter and studied it for a couple of minutes. I soon realized that watching it wouldn't do any good, so I decided to try to get some sleep and figure it out in the morning. Would I be able to sleep after this? Van and I snuggled under the covers. Had that crack always been in the ceiling? Maybe I need to repair it. I examined the ceiling for what seemed like forever while Van slept.

With every sound I jumped. Several times I got up and checked out the window. Occasionally, I noticed other vendors doing stuff at their trailers, but no one was around mine. I wasn't sure what time I'd fallen asleep, but I knew I hadn't gotten many hours. It would be hard to struggle through the day with the lack of sleep, but I had to push forward.

Not only was I concerned with finding out who had left the note, but I needed to finish some paintings. The note could be life or death, but no paintings to sell could be life or death too, as in, I'd have no money for food. Where was Ama this morning? I had expected her to appear right when I woke up. So far there'd been no sign of her. Van and I finished breakfast and stepped outside into the early-morning sun, which had just popped over the horizon, sending streaks of red and purple across the eastern sky.

"What a beautiful day, Van," I said.

My mind was still on the note. I'd shoved it into my pocket. I wasn't sure when I should notify Pierce or Caleb. Should I wait for a bit longer to make sure they were awake? I'd made it through the night, so maybe I was just worrying over nothing. If the killer wanted me, wouldn't he have tried to come after me already?

Furthermore, I wasn't sure whom to tell about this first. Both Caleb and Pierce would be upset if I told the other one first. Maybe I should text them at the same time. Yes, that was exactly what I should do. I pulled out my phone and wrote them a text.

I'm not sure if this is something to worry about, but I received a strange note in my trailer last night. Someone had slipped it under the door. Could it have been Danny? I saved the note. The person said they knew what I'd done.

What did the person mean when they said that? Was it Danny referring to me snooping around his trailer? Yes, that had to be it. It must have infuriated him to see us by his trailer.

"Are you ready?" the female voice called out.

When I spun around, I spotted Ama. She stood by the edge of the trailer, peeking around as if someone might see her.

I hurried over so that I could disguise talking to her better.

"Ready for what?" I asked.

"You have to go to the river and paint," she said. "I think you'll get the answers you need there."

She wasn't giving up on this. I had to admit that I was curious.

"Can't I just paint here?"

She shook her head. "It won't be the same. You need the energy from the river."

Since it was still early, I had time. "Okay, but I can't stay long."

Ama moved over to the path and motioned for me to join her. I left Van in the trailer and grabbed my canvas and paints. I hoped Caleb and Pierce didn't discover what I'd done. Following Ama, I walked along the wooded path toward the river. Every time a tree branch cracked under my foot, I jumped. Only the sound of the swaying tree branches and a few chatty birds filled the air. Light broke through the dim area when I came to the river clearing. The morning sun trickled over the water, glistening and dancing.

"This is the perfect spot. I sat in this spot many times when I was a little girl."

I sat on the ground and got out my paints. I tried to focus on the painting only, but it was tough, knowing that the killer could be out there. No matter how hard I tried not to, I kept glancing over my shoulder to make sure that no one was approaching.

"Don't worry, Celeste. If someone comes here, I will tell you," Ama said.

I wasn't sure if that mattered. Would it give me enough time to get away?

The image came to me quickly. In my mind, a man appeared. Feathers adorned his head, along with a fringed cloth tunic and a woven belt around his waist. Tall moccasins covered his feet.

I had no idea about the man's identity, but I painted him anyway. Ama waited back by the path so that she could alert me if someone was approaching. I dipped my paintbrush into the different colors, filling in the background around the man. The scowl on his face became apparent the more I painted. His dark eyes were so vivid it seemed as if he might pop out of the painting at any second. I painted lush green trees and used dark blue for the murky water of the river. This was another image of the river. Who was this man? Would Ama know him?

Ama saw me and approached. "What did you paint?"

Before I had a chance to respond, she peered down at the canvas. I could tell by her expression that she knew this man.

"Who is he?" I asked.

A line creased between her brows. "In English . . . he's called Grandfather."

"Wow. He's your grandfather?"

"That's him," she said.

Why had I painted her grandfather? Based on her expression, I assumed she wasn't happy about this.

"Is everything okay, Ama? I thought you'd be happy to see a painting of your grandfather."

"I knew he would come for me." She paced along the edge of the river.

"What do you mean?" I asked.

"My grandfather didn't want me to come back here. He tried to stop me. When he wasn't paying attention, I slipped out." She made a gesture with her hand indicating how fast she had moved on her way out.

"You mean he didn't want you to come back to this dimension?"

I was confused by all this ghostly stuff and had no idea how it worked. Was there some lengthy process to coming back from the spirit world?

"Yes, he thought I should have stayed in the spirit world. He'll probably try to come back and get me," she said.

I peeked around again to see if he'd made an appearance from the painting. So far, there was no sign of him. Was he hiding from us?

"Stop, not another brushstroke. You shouldn't paint him anymore." Ama stepped in front of my painting.

She held her arms out to her sides. The brush went right through her stomach.

"Oh, I am sorry, Ama," I said with widened eyes. "I didn't mean to stick the brush through you."

I hoped it hadn't hurt. Wait. She was a ghost. Of course, it didn't hurt. Sometimes momentarily I forgot such things.

"That's all right." She peered down at her stomach as if to check for damage.

"Why don't you want me to finish the painting? Don't you want to see your grandfather?" I asked.

Was it because if the painting was finished, he would come through? There had to be a reason she didn't want to see him.

"He's stubborn, and I don't want to speak with him." She crossed her arms in front of her waist. "I don't have to talk to him if I don't want to."

"Why do you say he's stubborn?"

I sensed that Ama and her grandfather were a lot alike.

"We argue about my use of the spirit world. Like I said, he doesn't want me to come through."

This wasn't the first time she'd made a visit back to the world of the living.

I placed my brush down. "Okay, if you don't want me to paint him anymore, I won't do it. However, you said coming here would be good. Maybe I'm meant to paint him for a reason."

The snap of a tree branch captured our attention. My breath caught in my throat.

"What was that?" I whispered.

"It was probably just the wind snapping a tree branch," Ama said, although she didn't sound convinced.

I hoped she was right, but how could I be sure?

I grabbed up my supplies. "I don't think I want to hang around any longer to find out if it was just the wind."

What if the killer was out there watching me? He could attack at any moment. What was I thinking by coming out here alone? I was putting myself at risk, and that was stupid. Just so that I could use the energy from the river for a stronger connection to the spirit world? There had to be a better way, though I had no idea what it was at the moment.

Ama followed me as I headed up the path toward the festival area. Another sound came from behind, and I whipped around for a better view. My breathing was heavy now, and my heart rate went up. All the trees around me made it hard to make out if a person was there. Another movement came from the left, and I gasped. A squirrel hopped across the path and jumped onto a nearby tree branch.

I clutched my chest. "Whew, it was just a little furry creature."

Ama's eyes widened, and I knew someone was behind me. Fear raced through my body as I spun around to see who had appeared. My neighbor Karla was now standing in front of me.

She scowled. "What are you doing?"

"I was painting by the river." I gestured over my shoulder.

Why was she making me nervous? I didn't have to answer her questions.

"Don't you know it's dangerous out here?" She narrowed her eyes.

If it was so dangerous out here, what was she doing walking along the path?

"I am well aware of the dangers," I said. "What about you? Why are you here?"

She eyed me up and down. "I saw you come back here and wanted to see what you were doing."

It had been some time since I'd come back to the river. Why had it taken her so long to come find me? I wasn't buying her excuse.

"What took you so long? I've been back here for at least twenty minutes."

She kept quiet, not uttering a word. Placing my hands on my hips, I waited for her answer. Without saying a word, she spun around and headed toward the festival area.

"That was strange," Ama said.

"Yes, it was odd. I don't know what she's up to,

but I should keep my eye on her. Something about her gives me the creeps," I said.

A few seconds later, Ama and I stepped out into the sunshine. People had already arrived for the fair. I needed to get my paintings set up in a hurry.

"Celeste," the male voice called out.

"Celeste, over here," another man said.

Caleb and Pierce were headed my way. I'd almost forgotten about texting them. Of course, they seemed panicked.

When I approached the trailer, they said in unison, "What are you doing coming out of that area?"

Had they practiced talking in sync?

I gestured toward the canvas and brushes in my hand. "Painting?"

"Are you kidding?" they said.

I grimaced.

"After receiving a threatening note, you decide to go back to the scene of a murder?" Caleb asked.

"With a killer on the loose?" Pierce asked.

What they wanted to add was "How dumb can you be?" Apparently pretty dumb.

"I'm fine. Plus, I wasn't technically at the scene of the murder. That area is much less secluded," I said. "I think the note was probably from Danny. I think he saw me at his trailer and wanted to warn me to stay away."

"This is nothing to mess around with, Celeste," Caleb said.

"And nothing to take lightly," Pierce added.

"What he said." Caleb gestured toward Pierce with a tilt of his head.

"Do you have the note?" Pierce asked.

I pulled it from my pocket and handed it to him. "I found it on the trailer floor. I guess he slipped it under the door."

He studied the note and, surprisingly, handed it to Caleb.

"We'll take that as evidence," Pierce said. "In the meantime, will you please stay away from dangerous areas?"

"It's my opinion that all areas are dangerous."

Caleb raised an eyebrow. "Well, some more than others. But why don't you just stick to areas that have people around?"

"You'll let me know right away if you get another note?" Pierce asked.

"Of course," I said. "I let you know right away when I received this one, didn't I?"

"And stop poking around for evidence or clues, Celeste. You're not Jessica Fletcher. This is your last warning," Pierce said with a stern voice.

I raised an eyebrow. "I'll take care of myself."

"Uh oh, I think he said the wrong thing," Ama said.

"If you all will excuse me, I have to get to work." I moved around them with my head held high.

I didn't give the men a chance to say anything else. My blood boiled. Yes, it was dangerous, but I couldn't just sit around and do nothing. Not when I had Ama and my secret images to guide the way. I stepped inside my trailer for a bit so that the men would take a hint and leave. I wanted them to know that I was upset and that I meant business.

After a couple of minutes, I stepped over to the tiny window and peered out. Caleb and Pierce were nowhere in sight. Thank goodness, they had gone. I didn't want to discuss this anymore. I guess they'd taken my not-so-subtle hint. Now it really was time for me to get to work.

"I'll be back for you in just a bit, Van," I said.

He licked his paws.

"I guess you told them," Ama said.

"I hate that I had to get mad, but it was the only option."

"You're right. Don't let them tell you what to do." Ama pumped her fist.

"Though I suppose they are worried about my safety," I said.

"And rightfully so," Ama said.

"And what about the fact that you're the one who wanted me to go to the river?"

"Everyone makes mistakes."

CHAPTER 11

*Network with other vendors. Maybe you can
share customers. Or clues.*

As the day unfolded, I kept busy talking with customers and even sold a couple of paintings. However, that didn't mean that the murder wasn't on my mind. It was at the edge of my thoughts—always there, as a reminder that things weren't safe.

My mother had insisted that I come to dinner tonight, even though I'd told her I was terribly busy. She reminded me that I was never too busy for family. I supposed I needed to visit and see what kinds of disasters my father had gotten into lately. My mother said she'd found a stash of doughnuts hidden in his truck. Considering he was diabetic, this was a big no-no. I'd have to have another talk with him. It was always in one ear and out the other, though.

After the incident this morning, I'd kept my eye on Karla. I'd never noticed that scar on her hand before. I wondered how she'd gotten it.

Perhaps from an incident down by the river where she'd killed Erica. Okay, I was probably overreacting, but the police always searched for wounds on the perpetrator that might be signs that they had committed the crime. Should I ask her how she'd gotten the scar on her hand? That would be an awkward conversation. Especially since she hadn't acted all that friendly toward me this morning.

Now that the fair was wrapping up for the day, maybe I could go over and talk with Karla again. I'd thank her for coming to check on me. After all, it was nice of her to think of me, even though she'd acted strangely and I was suspicious of her. What if she had been sincere and I had treated her rudely? Yes, an apology was definitely in order.

I put all the paintings away, took Van to the trailer for a nap, and headed over toward Karla's trailer. She hadn't noticed that I was approaching her. My anxiety ramped up since I didn't know how she would react to my visit. Just as I was a few steps away, she spotted me. Immediately she scowled. Apparently, she wasn't happy to see me.

I stepped over to her. "Karla, I just wanted to stop by and thank you for coming to check on me this morning. Clearly you were just worried about me, and I should have thanked you instead questioning you over your motives."

She studied my face as if she was trying to figure out if I was being sincere.

"You're welcome," she said with hostility in her voice.

She wasn't much of a talker. I'd have to work hard to get this conversation moving.

"We really do have to watch out for each other," I said.

She eyed me up and down. "Yes, I suppose we do."

Her words were filled with anger. She was clearly still upset with me. I wasn't sure how much information I'd be able to get out of her. Noticing her hand, I pretended that this was the first time I'd seen the injury. Maybe she didn't want to talk about it. I had scars of my own from knee surgeries. I never tried to hide them since I figured they were a part of me and showed that I was living life. I felt a bit nosy asking, though. Perhaps I should just mind my own business.

Karla had apparently noticed me checking out her scar.

"I had a car accident a while back. Then the other day I fell and scratched up the old wound." She moved her arm as if now she didn't want me to look at it.

I diverted my attention. "I'm sorry to hear that. I hope you're feeling better."

Was she telling the truth? Had she simply fallen, or was this an injury sustained from a struggle with Erica? Why would Karla kill Erica, though? As far as I knew, they didn't know each other before meeting here at the arts and craft fair.

"Thank you," she said as she went back to her art.

She wasn't paying attention to me now, and I

assumed that was her way of saying she was finished with this conversation.

"Well, thanks again," I said.

"Sure thing," she said, busying herself with mixing paint.

I headed back toward my trailer. Checking the time on my phone, I realized that most places in town were closing. I'd wanted to go by the library and do some research. Plus, I thought I would see if I could find a few people who knew Karla. Oh well. Maybe it was for the best. I was supposed to be at my parents' house soon. Although I needed to find out more about Erica. What did she do in her spare time? What was her life like? Knowing more about her would probably lead me to the killer.

Once back in my trailer, I snuggled with Van before it was time to leave for my parents' house. I had to build up my energy to deal with all the hijinks that were likely to occur. I pulled out my phone, wondering what I'd find if I searched Karla's name. Probably nothing, but I supposed it wouldn't hurt to take a peek.

I typed Karla Dean into my phone. Nothing came up right away, but when I scrolled down just a bit, I saw a news article about a car accident. I assumed it was the one Karla had referenced. I clicked on the link so that I could read the full article. I hadn't expected what I found.

Karla hadn't been alone in the car. Her sister had been in the car with her and had died in the crash. How horrible. Now I felt even worse for asking about her scar. I should just keep my nose out of things and my mouth shut. The biggest shock came when I saw the name of the person who had hit the car that Karla had been driving. Erica was listed as the driver of the other vehicle. My mouth dropped open in shock.

Did Karla feel that Erica was responsible for her sister's death? The article stated that the police hadn't charged Erica after the accident. It had been just that, an accident. It seemed as if there was nothing that Erica could have done to avoid it. Was Karla trying to get revenge? I wasn't sure what to think.

My time had run out. I had to get to my parents' house. I'd research this more later. Picking up Van, I headed out the door. When I took out the key to lock the door, I spotted a piece of paper taped to my trailer. I pulled it off and read it.

I won't warn you again.

I spun around to see if the person who'd left the note was still anywhere around. People were at their booths, but no one was paying attention to me. That didn't mean the person responsible wasn't somewhere close, though. Karla was at her booth.

She must have sensed me watching her. After a couple of seconds of staring, she moved away. Checking to my right, I spotted Danny at his trailer. He watched me for a brief bit too. It had to be him who'd left the note. I should confront him. I'd let him know that I wasn't scared of him, though in all actuality, I was. Why would he leave a second note? I hadn't been around his trailer again.

Collecting all my courage, I marched toward his trailer. When he saw me walking his way, he diverted his attention, as though somehow now he didn't want to make eye contact.

With my shoulders pressed back and my head held high, I stepped up to him. "Why are you leaving me these notes?"

I waved the paper.

He casually wiped off his paintbrush. "I don't know what you're talking about. Are you crazy or something? All that pink has gotten to your brain."

I narrowed my eyes. "Don't play dumb with me. I know you left this note. And now I want to know why."

"I know your boyfriends probably put you up to this, but I had nothing to do with that girl's murder. You all need to leave me alone," he said.

"They're not my boyfriends," I said. "We're friends. They know about the first note you left. And now I'm going to show them this one."

He jumped up from his chair and closed the distance between us within seconds. Now he stood inches away from me with his face right in front of mine.

"Listen to me. You leave me alone, or you will regret it," he said through gritted teeth.

I'd never seen so much anger from someone. I backed away, unsure if he was ready to punch me. After a couple of seconds, I spun around and headed back my trailer. His threat wouldn't stop me from telling Caleb and Pierce about this. I'd done nothing to Danny to warrant a second threatening note. Or a first one, for that matter.

Based on his anger, I had to assume he was the one who'd left the notes. I didn't even want to see if he was watching me or, heaven forbid, following me. Karla watched me again now too. She'd probably witnessed the whole scene with Danny. A slight grin appeared on her face before she finally went back to her craft work.

Maybe going to my parents' house right now would be a good thing. I needed a break from the fair. I gathered up Van and his supplies from the trailer, and we hopped into the truck.

"Let's get out of here, Van. Do you want to see your Pappy and Mamaw?" I asked.

He covered his eyes with his paws.

"Yes, I know they're a bit quirky, but we love them." I shoved the truck into DRIVE and pulled away from the fair.

I had the note with me, and I intended on letting Caleb and Pierce know about it as soon as possible. They probably wouldn't believe me and would think that I'd been messing around Danny's trailer again. They had to believe me at some point, though. It wasn't like I failed to mention the truth that often. I always came clean when I'd done something they didn't like.

As I drove down the road toward my parents' house, I released a deep breath. It felt good to be away from the stress for a few minutes. Up ahead was the psychic's place that I'd gone to with my best friend, Samantha Sutton—or Sammie, as everyone called her. I felt I needed to stop in once again. Maybe Madame Gerard could help me with all of this.

According to the truck's dashboard clock, I had a bit of time to stop at the psychic's place before I had to be at my parents' house. They'd be upset if I was late, so I couldn't stay long. Maybe Madame Gerard wasn't even seeing clients right now.

I pulled into the driveway and cut the engine. "Okay, Van, we're here to see Madame Gerard. You like her, remember?"

Again, he placed his paws up to his eyes as if he didn't want to see.

"It's okay, we won't see any scary ghosts this time." I picked him up and climbed out of the truck.

"Where are we?" Ama asked as she walked along beside me.

"Madame Gerard is a psychic medium. She talks to the spirit world. I bet she'll be able to speak with you too." I stepped up to the door.

The neon OPEN sign blinked. Other signs depicting palm reading and tarot cards covered the windows.

"You can see me and talk to me. Are you a psychic medium?" Ama asked.

I pushed on the doorbell. "Maybe. I guess I never thought about it."

After a couple of minutes, the familiar sound of multiple locks clicking came from the other side of the door. I wasn't sure why Madame Gerard felt she needed so many. What was she keeping out or in? The door eased open just an inch, and she peeked out around the edge. Our eyes met. Within seconds, she opened the door. The faintest of grins crossed her lips. I assumed that meant that she was happy to see me.

"Celeste, please come in," she said with a wave of her hand.

Maybe Madame Gerard liked me after all.

Ama followed me as I stepped through the door. Surprisingly, Madame Gerard hadn't acted as if she'd noticed Ama. I thought that would have been one of the first things she would have done. I'd brought a ghost to her door in the past, and she'd zoned in on the spirit right away. Maybe Madame Gerard was having an off day.

Madame Gerard gestured toward the room to the right, where she conducted all her supernatural business. A large round table took up the space in the middle of the room. Chairs circled it, and a white tablecloth was draped over the top. A crystal ball sat in the middle of the table. Ama trailed behind me as I stepped into the room, but she remained quiet as she peered with wide eyes. Madame Gerard still hadn't noticed Ama. This was interesting. How long would it be until she picked up that there was a spirit in the room?

"Please have a seat, Celeste." Madame Gerard pointed.

I slipped down onto one of the chairs and placed Van in the one beside me. He sniffed the air in Madame Gerard's direction. She noticed him watching, and the right side of her mouth tilted up just a hint. As far as I knew, she wasn't one for displaying affection. Madame Gerard walked over to the antique mahogany cabinet in the corner of the room and opened the double doors, displaying an assortment of candles. She reached for a couple of white ones. Ama stood beside the table as if she was unsure what to do next.

I gestured with a wave of my hand toward the chair on my left side. "You can sit in this chair if you'd like."

Madame Gerard whipped around from the cabinet and focused her attention to the left of me. "Someone else is here."

"I wondered when you would realize that," I said.

Madame Gerard hurried back across the room and placed the candles on the table.

She narrowed her eyes. "Who is it?"

I studied Ama and said, "She came to me one day when I was painting down by the river. She lived on the land there."

"A restless soul," Madame Gerard said.

"She says she wants to help me find a killer, though I'm not sure why."

"I'm sensing her energy now." Madame Gerard closed her eyes. "She's here not only to help you. There's something else she needs."

Ama's brown eyes widened. "What is she talking about?"

"You've been in danger," Madame Gerard said.

"I'm not in danger," Ama said with a frown. "Am I in danger?"

"I don't think so," I said.

I knew Madame Gerard wasn't talking about Ama.

Madame Gerard opened her eyes. "Not the spirit. You. Celeste. You're in danger."

"Why am I in danger?"

I had asked, although I probably knew the answer already, considering there was a killer running around and I was seeking that killer. That had put me in a bit of hot water.

"You are after something," she said, staring into the crystal ball. "Or someone."

"Yes, I suppose you could say that," I said.

"But I think this something or someone you're seeking will find you first, and that's very dangerous."

I released an audible gasp. "You're saying I shouldn't try to track down this person?"

"No, you should not." She fixated squarely on me.

Would I follow her warning? In my mind, I didn't have a choice. Besides, how dangerous could it be? Policemen were watching the fair. And I wasn't doing anything too dangerous, just kind of snooping around a little.

"What makes you think it's so dangerous?" I asked.

"The person you're searching for is evil, and I don't think they will tolerate much more of you snooping around."

"Do you see this person in the crystal ball?" I pointed to it.

She waved her hands. "No, when someone is bad, all I see is a silhouette, as if the evil blocks out the features. Sometimes I'm able to get it to come through, but it takes a while, and it's very draining."

"You will let me know if you do find out?" I asked.

"I will absolutely let you know, but you will take my warning, right?" she asked.

"Yes, I will take your warning," I said.

I had just lied to her, because I wasn't going to take the warning seriously. Well, maybe seriously, but that didn't mean that I would stop searching for the killer. Sometimes life was dangerous and risks had to be taken.

"Do you see anything else?" I asked, leaning forward and gazing into the crystal ball as if I would actually see something too.

Madame Gerard peered into the ball again. "There is nothing there. I'm sorry."

CHAPTER 12

*You can barter with others. They might have
services they can trade in exchange for a
lovely haunted painting.*

Madame Gerard had warned me about what I
already knew. I had hoped for new information
about the killer.

"There was a murder at the craft festival. I
suppose you heard about that," I said.

"Yes, I heard. You are there, and the killer is
nearby."

I had assumed that as well, although hearing
it still sent a shiver down my spine.

"I want to find the killer before they have a
chance to do this to someone else," I said.

"The police are searching for the killer. I'm
not sure that you need to do it," she said.

Now she sounded like Caleb and Pierce.

"More help seems like a good thing to me," I
said.

"Not in this case." Madame Gerard focused
on me.

"Well, I guess I'd better go. I have to be at my parents' house." I stood up from the table.

"Tell your father to watch out for the hole that he dug in the backyard. He has a tendency to forget about the dangers around him," Madame Gerard said.

I knew that, in this case, she meant the dangers that he created for himself.

"I'll make sure to tell him. I doubt he'll listen, though," I said as I picked up Van.

Madame Gerard walked with me to the door. Ama trailed behind Madame Gerard. Once again, Madame Gerard had missed Ama. Either she wasn't using all her energy to pick up on Ama or Ama was just good at blocking out Madame Gerard. I wondered if Ama did that on purpose.

"Please be safe, Celeste," Madame Gerard said when I reached the door.

"I will," I said.

Madame Gerard watched as I walked back to my truck. She still hadn't seen Ama trailing along beside me or paid attention that she was still with me.

When we got in the truck, I asked, "Ama, are you intentionally hiding yourself from the psychic?"

"Not on purpose, but she didn't seem to notice me much." Ama beamed as if she was proud of her accomplishment.

"I guess some spirits are just trickier than others," I said with a wink.

We headed down the road toward my parents' house. Was Ama ever in for a treat when she met my family. I wasn't sure if I should warn her ahead of time or just let her experience them without any previous knowledge. Sometimes it was better to be blissfully unaware of what was about to happen. After meeting my family, I wouldn't be surprised if Ama left for good. I wouldn't say that I would blame her if she did.

As we neared my parents' house, I spotted smoke billowing into the sky. I knew right away that it had to be coming from their house.

"What do you think the smoke is for?" Ama asked.

"I have a feeling it's not good." I pushed the gas so that I would get there a bit sooner. Would the fire trucks be right behind me? When I pulled into the driveway, my brothers had something on fire in the front yard. I jumped out of the truck, leaving Van there for safekeeping until I could secure the area.

"What are you thinking? What are you doing?" I asked, putting my hands on my hips.

"Oh, hey, sis," my brother Stevie said. "We were just having a little experiment."

"One that's gone wrong, I see," I said.

Just then my mother came out the front door with the fire extinguisher. Ama stood beside me in shock. My mother calmly walked over to the fire. She doused the flames with the foam from the fire extinguisher.

She pointed a warning finger at my brothers. "Now knock it off."

Without saying a word to me, she just walked back into the house.

I went over and smacked Stevie on the shoulder. "What's the matter with you? Don't you think mom doesn't have enough to worry about with dad. She doesn't need you all adding to the stress. Now stop the nonsense."

"It was under control," my other brother Hank said. "You worry too much."

"Yeah, I worry about the house being burned down."

"Do they do this all the time?" Ama asked.

"Yes, they do," I said without thinking.

My brothers laughed, holding their stomachs for emphasis.

"She's lost it again." Stevie twirled his index finger next to his temple to demonstrate my level of insanity.

There was no way I wanted to tell them about Ama right now.

"Never mind," I said as I headed for the house.

I stepped inside and called out for my mother.

"In the kitchen," she yelled out when she heard the door.

Somehow, she'd always sensed when I would be around. It was like she had eyes in the back of her head. The smell of a mixture of foods filled the house. I knew there would be cornbread and pie. That was something that could be counted on at every family meal, as sure as the sun came up every day.

"Where's Dad?" I asked as I stepped into the room.

The message from the psychic still played in my mind.

"He's outside." My mother pointed toward the backyard.

I raced over to the back door and scanned the area. My father was walking across the backyard. Things were getting ready to play out exactly as the psychic had said they would.

"Dad, stop," I yelled.

"What in the world is going on?" my mother asked. "Why are you yelling?"

My father stopped in his tracks and peered over his shoulder. I ran out of the house and over to him.

"What's wrong?" he asked with a scrunched brow.

I pointed at the yard. "Don't you remember that hole you dug?"

He peered down. "I guess I was getting ready to step in it, huh?"

I pulled on his arm to put some distance between the hole and his foot.

"How did you know I was about to step in that?" he asked.

"I guess I just remembered," I said.

"You've got your mother's memory," he said.

"Good thing you saved your father," Ama said.

"What was that? Did you hear something? It sounded like a voice," my father said.

Had my father heard Ama?

"I'm not sure," I said.

He peered around. "Must have been your mother talking inside the house."

My mother was soft-spoken, and he knew it,

though she could be loud when it came to my brothers and my father. It was the only way they'd listen to her.

"Let's get inside for dinner," he said.

Ama followed us as we made our way across the yard to the kitchen door. My father scowled almost as if he sensed her. I'd never known him to pick up on anything supernatural. As a matter of fact, he never believed in that sort of thing. I wanted to tell him about the ghost, but he thought I was just using my vivid imagination anytime I mentioned the paranormal. I would just have to keep this to myself.

Delicious aromas struck me again as we neared the screen door. My mouth watered instantly. I didn't realize how hungry I was until I'd arrived. Van was in the kitchen, standing at my mother's feet as she prepared the food. I'd have to watch my dad because he always wanted to share food with Van. Then Van would end up with a bellyache.

My brothers burst through from the living room. Even though my mother tried to remind them of the table manners she'd taught them as children, they mostly ignored her instructions. At least they used silverware and napkins. That was probably as much as we could hope for from them. They sat down at the table and stuffed the napkins into the front of their shirt collars. They grabbed their forks and stabbed at the chicken breasts on the platter.

"Slow down, guys, the chickens are already dead," I said.

"Funny," my bother said as he slapped a pound of mashed potatoes onto his plate.

Ama stood by the kitchen door and watched the scene unfold. Would my family scare a ghost away? Watching my brothers' lack of table manners would be likely to frighten the paranormal world.

"What's going on at that craft fair?" my father asked as he reached for the potatoes.

My mother took them away after he went back for a second scoop.

"It's good. I've sold quite a few paintings," I said.

"Not that . . . I want to know about the murder and why you're still hanging around there," my father said.

"She's crazy, that's why," Stevie said.

"Don't talk about your sister like that," my mother warned.

"I have to sell my art," I said as I pushed the food around the plate with my fork.

"You don't want to die in the process," my father said.

"No, of course not. There are detectives there, so I think it's safe." I poked at my food with my fork.

"Oh, she thinks it's safe, so that should make us feel better," Hank said.

"Is one of the detectives Caleb?" my mother asked with a wink.

"I still don't know if I trust that guy. He wasn't truthful in the beginning," my father said, gesturing with his fork.

"He was undercover, so he couldn't tell me he was a detective," I said. "And yes, he is there now. Along with Pierce."

My parents had met Caleb. The fact that he still talked to me after meeting my family said something about Caleb. My family hadn't met Pierce yet. I had to pace myself with introducing them to friends.

"Pierce? What is he, a movie star?" Stevie asked.

I scowled. "No, he's with the FBI now."

Hank held his hands up. "I hope he doesn't arrest me."

I rolled my eyes. And they wondered why I didn't want to come to dinner.

"What are they doing to find the killer?" my father asked.

Thank goodness, he didn't know that I'd been trying to find the killer too. Plus, I didn't want them to know that I had received threatening notes. They would force me to leave the craft fair.

"They have been interviewing people," I said, trying to be vague.

"Like who?" my mother asked.

"They don't tell me the specifics," I said.

My mother raised an eyebrow. "I don't believe that. You talk to Caleb, and probably this Pierce, all the time. Plus, you are nosy. I've seen the text messages on your phone."

And she thought I was nosy?

"I am not nosy," I said defensively.

Her left eyebrow remained tilted up. My brothers and my father crossed their arms in front of their chests.

"Okay, I'm a little nosy."

They still watched me.

"Okay, I'm a lot nosy. Are you happy now?"

"I won't be happy until you're out of there." My father punctuated the sentence by pointing his fork at me.

My mother lifted an eyebrow, and I knew she wouldn't let the question go without an answer from me.

"Well, they've been interviewing a guy at the craft fair. He's a painter. He does a lot of dark, spooky art," I said.

"He sounds like a creep," Hank said.

"Pretty much," I said.

"I don't want you to have any dealings with this guy," my mother said.

"I don't," I said, studying my plate.

I knew if my mother saw my face, she'd read my expression. She'd know that I was keeping something from her. Silence fell over the room. Even the sound of my brothers scarfing down food had stopped. I knew they all had suspicions about my involvement with the investigation.

"Are you going to tell us the truth now?" my mother asked.

"What about the truth?"

"Have you been snooping around the investigation?" my mother asked.

They seemed to forget that I had been an adult for a number of years now.

"I'm just there trying to sell paintings," I said. "Now, can we change the subject?"

My mother quirked an eyebrow. My father scowled. My brothers continued eating.

"So what do you plan on setting on fire next?" I asked, changing the subject to my brothers' shenanigans.

CHAPTER 13

*Don't be afraid to ask for help with customers
if you need it. Also, maybe they can help with
the ghosts and locating a killer.*

The craft fair got another sunny start this morning, and I'd convinced my best friend, Sammie, to watch the booth for me while I went to the library.

"You want me to sit here like a sitting duck and wait for the killer to show up?" she'd asked with wide eyes.

"Don't be ridiculous," I said. "It's daylight, and there are a bunch of people around. Nothing will happen to you. Just don't go into that wooded area over there."

"If I'm murdered, I will come back to haunt you. I will be relentless."

"I have no doubt," I said.

Sammie had been reluctant to stay but finally agreed. I took off for the library, leaving her there with Van. I was confident that she would be just fine. I knew Caleb was around, although

I hadn't seen Danny this morning, which was kind of odd. Usually, I caught him staring at me. Karla had been at her booth, keeping an eye on my movements as usual.

I pulled my truck up to the library and parked next to the entrance. I hopped out and headed inside, excited for what I might find. Sure, if I didn't find anything, I would be disappointed, but I kept positive thoughts in mind that I would have success. I felt positive thinking worked. No doubt, the thought of finding a clue was exciting.

The first things I wanted to check were newspaper articles. I wasn't sure how, but something was telling me that I should check for similar crimes. It was a nagging thought in the back of my mind.

Only a few patrons sat around the tables in the middle of the room. The librarian wasn't around. I sat down at the table and sorted through some articles. I checked recent news, but nothing was showing up as suspicious or remotely connected. I wanted to find out if there was anything in the area or to possibly see a mention of Erica's name.

A couple of minutes later, I'd found more articles about the horrible car accident. Erica had been involved in about a year ago. I remembered hearing about this on the news at the time.

Maybe it was my imagination, but the photo of the surviving crash victim looked a lot like the Karla who was in the booth nearby to mine. I leaned closer to the screen for better scrutiny.

Yes, it had to be Karla. Why had she not mentioned this to me? Right away I became suspicious. Was she trying to hide this? Did Pierce
and Caleb know about this? I stopped myself
from picking up my phone and calling them
right away. I had to make sure it was Karla first.

When I scrolled down the screen and saw the
other name that had been involved in the accident, I almost fell out of my chair. Erica's car
had been the one who'd hit someone else's car.
And unfortunately, someone in that car had
died. But the driver of the car that Erica hit was
Karla Dean. I was right. It had been her, and
she'd never spoken a word about it. This would
be a huge deal, considering she'd acted as if she
didn't know Erica.

Should I confront her with this information?
Why not? Yes, I should just come right out and
ask her. I'd tell her that I saw it in the newspaper. No, that wouldn't work since it had happened over a year ago. I'd just tell her that my
memory had been triggered and I'd remembered seeing her picture in the paper. Though if
she was the killer, that might trigger her and she
might try to kill me too. I'd just play it by ear
and see what happened.

I stood up from the computer and spun around
to leave. A flash of someone as they walked behind a bookshelf caught my attention, stopping
me in my tracks. I thought for sure I'd spotted
Danny. Had he followed me here? That thought
sent a shiver down my spine. Nevertheless, I had
to see if it was him. Why was he following me?

I walked over to the aisle where I'd just seen

him. When I peeked around the side, he wasn't there. He must have walked down the other side. My heart beat a little faster as I spun around to see if he was now behind me.

Thank goodness, he wasn't there. Had I imagined this? No, I knew for sure I'd seen him. Though maybe it was just someone who looked like him. After all, I'd only gotten a glimpse of the man. I hoped it really wasn't Danny. The thought that he was following me gave me the creeps.

I walked around the other shelves but still didn't see him. I released a breath of relief. It must have just been someone else, and now the person had left the library. Or it really was Danny and he'd left in a hurry once he knew I'd seen him. I needed to get out of here. If he was following me, I'd have to be on guard as I left the building. When I stepped out of the library, I surveyed all around for any sign of Danny.

He was nowhere in sight, so I hurried to my truck. If he had been searching for me, it would certainly be easy to track me down with my pink truck. It stuck out like a neon sign. Perhaps I should borrow someone else's car for a while. Could I afford to get a rental car until all of this was settled?

After jumping in the truck, I pulled out of the library parking lot. As I cruised down the road, I caught a glimpse of a car behind me. It was close, and I recognized it right away. Now I had my answer for sure. Danny was behind the steering wheel and was trailing close to my bumper. My adrenaline pumped. What would I do now?

It was too dangerous to reach for my phone in my purse. I would have to drive somewhere safe. I'd watched a program about a woman who'd been run off the road and kidnapped. I didn't want to meet that same fate.

I was still a good distance from the police station, and I wasn't sure I could make it there before Danny tried something crazy. Up ahead was a traffic light, and I prayed that it wouldn't change to red. Would he get out of his car and approach my truck? Did I have anything to use as a weapon if he attacked me? How dare he follow me like this? Not only was I scared, but now I was angry too.

Thank goodness, the red light didn't catch me. I cruised through under the green light, but soon realized that Danny had made a right. Relief washed over me, though I was still cautious and reeling from the experience. Maybe he hadn't been following me after all. No. I felt sure he'd done that on purpose. Maybe he was just trying to scare me. It had worked, but I wouldn't let on to him that I was scared.

My phone alerted me that I had a text message. I'd have to wait to read it, though, because I didn't want to take a chance and pull over. Danny could reappear at any time. Now what would I do? Should I tell Caleb and Pierce about my encounter with Danny? Or was it really nothing to worry about? At the least, I had to tell them what I'd discovered about Karla and Erica. Though they probably already knew. Why didn't they tell me these things?

I really wanted to confirm that Karla was the

same person listed in the newspaper article. Though since the photo had looked just like Karla Dean, I was almost certain. I'd have to think of a sly way to ask her. If I came right out and asked, she'd be suspicious. She probably already questioned my motives.

Thank goodness, I safely pulled up to the craft fair and parked the truck. As I walked back toward the booths, I kept my eye out for anything or anyone acting suspiciously. At this point, I couldn't trust anyone. When I reached the edge of Karla's trailer, I paused. She was probably around at the front working on her leather bags. Standing at the edge of the trailer, I released a deep breath.

Working up my courage, I peeked around the side. I hoped she didn't see me doing this. Karla was nowhere in sight. Thank goodness, she wasn't standing right behind me. That would have given me a heart attack. She wasn't beside me either. Thank goodness. Now I wasn't sure what to do next. I had no plan.

After a few more seconds, I stepped out from around Karla's trailer. She'd left all her items out. There were no customers around; it was kind of a slow time right now. I spotted Sammie at my booth. She was talking with a customer and had no idea that I was anywhere around.

I peered down and spotted a black wallet on the ground by Karla's trailer door. Moving closer, I reached down and picked it up. I opened it to check for identification. Someone had obviously lost their wallet. When I saw the picture and name, I realized this was Karla's wallet. I peered around again to see if I spotted Karla. Still she was nowhere around. Now at least I had confirmed that she was the woman who had been in the accident.

"What do you think you're doing?" the female voice yelled.

I spun around to see Karla approaching me. Uh oh. I was in trouble now.

"Are you stealing from me?" She closed the distance between us quickly.

Before I had a chance to answer, she yanked the wallet from my hands.

"Of course, I'm not stealing from you. I happened to walk by and saw the wallet on the ground. I didn't want anyone to take it, so I picked it up," I said defensively.

How dare she accuse me of stealing?

"I saw you rifling through it. You were trying to take the money out."

"If I was trying to do that, do you really think I'd stand right here to do it?" I placed my hands on my hips.

She narrowed her eyes. "I'm not sure what you're capable of."

"What's that supposed to mean?" I asked.

"You found the murdered woman." Karla raised an eyebrow. "What's to say that you didn't kill her?"

"Is that right? What's to say *you* didn't kill her?" I tossed it back to her.

She scoffed. "That's preposterous. Why would I do that? I can't believe you have the audacity to accuse me of something like that."

"You knew Erica, and you're acting as if you didn't," I said.

I hadn't planned on confronting her with this, but she'd left me no choice. I wasn't going to let her accuse me of something so horrendous.

She eyed me up and down, seemingly growing nervous. "What makes you say that?"

Karla's voice cracked. There was no way she could get out of this one. I'd confront her with the newspaper article if I had to.

"I know you had a car accident with Erica last year. I'm sorry your sister died in the wreck, but I know that Erica was the one driving the car that hit yours."

Her face reddened. "You don't know anything."

Without waiting for another response from me, she stormed past me and walked into her trailer. She slammed the door shut, leaving me standing alone. This had caught the attention of several people, including Sammie. She held her arms up as if to ask what I was doing. I hated that I might have upset Karla by mentioning her sister's death. Maybe I should have kept quiet. I hurried over to my booth, where Sammie was waiting for me.

"What was that all about?" she asked.

I blew the hair out of my eyes. "Where do I start? Number one, Karla accused me of trying to steal her wallet."

Sammie scowled. "Why would she do that?"

"Well, I was holding her wallet when she walked up to her booth," I said.

Sammie raised an eyebrow. "I have to admit that's not good, Celeste. Why were you holding her wallet?"

"I found it on the ground by her trailer. I thought someone had lost it, and I was just trying to be helpful," I said.

"That makes sense, but why were you by her trailer?" Sammie asked.

"Snooping around, of course."

"That could be dangerous. What are you snooping for?"

So far there was no sign of Karla. Thank goodness, she hadn't come back out of her trailer yet.

"This is something bad, isn't it?" Sammie asked.

"I did some research, and you're not going to believe what I discovered at the library."

Sammie's eyes widened. "What did you discover?"

"About a year ago, Karla was involved in a car accident with Erica."

"Erica? The woman who was murdered?" Sammie asked.

"Yes, that Erica. According to the report, Erica hit Karla's car. It was a horrific crash, and Karla's sister died. The police said it was just a horrible accident because of wet roads."

"That is awful," Sammie said. "But you think that Karla might have been out for revenge, don't you?"

"I'm certainly not ruling it out as a possibility," I said.

"Did you ask her about it?"

"She left me no choice really. She accused me of killing Erica."

"How did that happen?" Sammie asked.

"She basically implied that, if I was capable of stealing her wallet, I was capable of killing someone too."

"That could just be a distraction to throw you off her trail," Sammie said.

"That's what I thought," I said.

"Have you told Caleb or Pierce about this?" Sammie asked.

"No, but I'm definitely going to tell them now," I said.

"They won't like your snooping around," Sammie said in a singsong voice.

CHAPTER 14

Watch your body language. People might mis-interpret your actions. Don't shout or be too quiet either. It's best not to arouse suspicions.

Darkness had fallen over the craft fair. Instead of hiding out in my trailer because there was a killer on the loose, I decided to go out into the scary world and hunt for him. At least, I didn't go to the river. I wasn't that crazy. However, I had decided to visit Madame Gerard. I knew that she accepted customers until nine-thirty. It was nine now. If I hurried, I could get there before she closed. Somehow, I'd convinced Sammie to tag along. I hadn't wanted to go alone, and having Ama with me wasn't enough. Everyone else would still think I was alone. I felt safer if people saw me with someone.

Sammie had left the craft fair this afternoon, but she had agreed to come back, picking me up in the church's parking lot. As I walked toward the lot, every rustle of a leaf or chirp of a cricket made me antsy. As I hurried toward the spot where Sammie was supposed to meet me, I held Van in my arms. He'd walked on his leash for a short distance, but he'd decided he'd rather I carry him.

Unfortunately, Sammie's car wasn't there when I arrived. I hoped I didn't have to wait long for her. A few cars were parked around the lot, but there were no people. It felt as if someone watched me as I stood there. I peered around to see if maybe I was missing someone, but I still saw no one around. I pulled out my phone and sent Sammie a text message.

Where are you? It's scary out here.

I'd barely hit SEND when I spotted her car pull into the parking lot. I released a deep breath. Thank goodness, she'd shown up. When she pulled up, I hopped in right away.

She checked her phone and read my text. "It's scary out here? Maybe you should think about that before you decide to play detective and get me involved too."

"I took that into consideration," I said.

"Yet it didn't stop you," Sammie said as she took off across the lot.

"You'd think it would, but it didn't."

Sammie still hadn't seen Ama, which surprised me a bit since I knew Sammie had seen a ghost before. Ama sat in the middle of the back seat and leaned forward so she could hear our conversation. I checked the time on my phone. It was now eight minutes after nine, and we still had a five-minute drive.

"We have to hurry if we want to get there before she closes," I said.

"What made you decide to see the psychic tonight?" Sammie asked as she pulled out onto the street.

"Just a feeling, I guess. Something was drawing me to her," I said.

"You'd better hope she feels the same way or she won't be happy with this last-minute visit," Sammie said as she sped through a yellow light.

"You're telling me. Have you noticed how her dark eyes penetrate right through you?"

"It sends a shiver down my spine." Sammie shook.

"I don't have to worry about that since she can't even see me," Ama said. "Are you sure she's even gifted with the spirit world?"

I wasn't sure if I should answer Ama and tell Sammie about her now. Maybe I should wait until after we'd seen the psychic, though Madame Gerard would likely mention sensing that Ama was around. I'd might as well come clean now.

"What are you inspecting back there?" Sammie asked. "I know I need to clean my car, but you don't need to criticize."

"It's not that," I said.

"Well, what is it?" Sammie asked, taking her eyes off the road for just a second.

"There's a ghost in your back seat." I gestured with a tilt of my head.

She swerved, and the car in the lane next to us honked. Perhaps I should have told her a different way. Or waited until we were parked.

"Oh, my gosh, Celeste. What's going on? Are we in danger? Do I need to pull the car over?"

"No need to pull over. I know who the ghost is," I said.

"Who?" Sammie asked breathlessly.

"I met her at the river when I was painting. Her name is Ama. She used to live on the land where the church is now."

"Interesting." Sammie peeked into the rear-view mirror, hoping to see Ama. "Is she nice?"

"She's super nice," I said.

"Thank you, Celeste," Ama said as she leaned forward in the seat.

"She doesn't know why she's here, though." Shifting in the seat slightly, I kept my eye on Ama.

"Maybe Madame Gerard can answer that question for you," Sammie said.

"I doubt it. I was here the other day, and she didn't even see Ama," I said. "Which is weird because I thought Madame Gerard was able to see when a ghost is around."

"You already came to see Madame Gerard?" Sammie's voice rose. "Why didn't you tell me about this?"

I nervously tapped my fingers against the seat. "It was a spur of the moment thing. I guess I didn't think anything of it."

"What did she say?"

I hesitated before answering. "She just said that I was in danger."

"What? See. I knew you were messing with things you shouldn't mess with. I think you should quit that craft fair right away."

"I can't just quit. Plus, I think we'll figure out who did this soon," I said.

"If Madame Gerard didn't give you any helpful information, why are we going back again?" Sammie asked.

"It's just a feeling I have, I suppose. Something tells me she might have information for me this time."

"It's kind of like you're psychic too." Excitement filled Ama's voice.

Soon we arrived at Madame Gerard's place. There was only one tiny light on in the cottage-style house, though the neon OPEN sign was still lit up against the dark night. We all hurried out of the car and raced up the path toward her front door.

"We still have five minutes to spare," I said, checking the time on my phone.

"I hope she answers the door," Sammie said. "I think she'll be unhappy with you that you waited until right before she stops for the night."

"I feel bad about that, but this is urgent," I said.

Once in front of the door, I rang the bell. My heart beat faster as I wondered how Madame Gerard would react to seeing us on her front porch. Several seconds passed with no sound.

"Do you think she's already asleep?" I asked.

"She could be," Sammie said.

It felt as if someone was watching us. I saw an eye peeking out from the window. The rest of the face was covered by the lace curtains. Another few seconds went by, and the sound of locks rattling came from the other side of the door. The door opened just a bit. She didn't speak.

"Madame Gerard, I know it's late, but I was wondering if I could talk with you," I said.

My anxiety spiked as I thought she would tell me to go away and close the door in my face.

After a couple more seconds, she opened the door wider and said, "Come in."

Sammie grimaced. "I hope she doesn't yell at us."

We filed into the house and moved to the living room with the large round table. Without being instructed, we took seats around the table. Madame Gerard went to the candles and lit them. Smoke still came from some of them as if she'd only blown out the flame seconds earlier. She joined us at the table, taking a seat across from us. The crystal ball was still placed in the middle of the table. Van was on the seat beside me.

Madame Gerard eyed Sammie and me. She still hadn't noticed Ama.

"What is the reason for your visit tonight?" Madame Gerard asked. Before I had a chance to answer, she held her hand up. "Wait. I sense something."

She closed her eyes and placed her hands on the crystal ball. Sammie lifted an eyebrow, and I shrugged. I had no idea what Madame Gerard was sensing. She rubbed the ball, and after a few more seconds, she opened her eyes.

"You are in danger, but you have to go back to the river."

My eyes widened. "If I'm in danger, why would I want to go back to where I found the body? I assume you mean I'm in danger because of the killer who is still out there on the loose."

"There's something that you missed, and you have to go back to retrieve it," she said.

I didn't like the sound of this.

"If it's dangerous, why should I go back and put myself in danger?" I asked.

She narrowed her eyes. "Because it's important that you find this item."

"But can you tell me what it is?" I asked.

"No, I don't know what it is," she said.

"So I have to go to this dangerous place and comb around for something, but I have no idea what it is."

"Maybe I can help you." Ama leaned forward, trying to gaze into the crystal ball.

"You asked for my help, and I'm telling you what I see," Madame Gerard said with frustration in her voice.

Sammie touched my hand to let me know that I should just agree to this and leave.

"All right, I'll hunt for it," I said.

I didn't understand why Madame Gerard wanted me to go to the river and explore, but I just agreed instead of arguing.

"Do you have any other clues for me? Like where exactly I might find the item?" I asked.

She peered into the crystal ball again. I waited on pins and needles, hoping that she would have some clues for me other than the vague-sounding things she had said.

Madame Gerard opened her eyes again. "No, I have nothing."

Well, that was anticlimactic.

"I suppose we'll leave you alone now. I'm sorry I came so late," I said.

"Wait just a minute," she said, holding up her hand.

"Yes?" I said, sitting back down.

Maybe she'd figured out something else to tell me that was worthwhile.

Madame Gerard focused directly on Ama. "Why didn't you tell me about her sooner?"

She had seen her. "I wondered when you would notice she was here. She was here last time as well."

Madame Gerard scowled. "You should've told me sooner."

"I figured there was no reason if you didn't see her," I said.

Madame Gerard seemed upset that she had missed the ghost until now. Maybe she felt that was putting her expertise in doubt. I couldn't help it if the ghost was hiding from her.

"I found her at the river," I said.

Okay, that sounded as if I was talking about an object that I'd discovered.

"What I mean to say is that she found me. I think I painted her spirit here from another dimension."

"This is very odd," Madame Gerard said. "Very odd indeed."

I released a deep breath and leaned back in the chair. "Yes, it's strange. I don't understand it, and I don't think Ama does either."

"So there is a connection to that area where you picked up the spirit," Madame Gerard said.

"Now you should understand why I don't want go back there."

"But do you understand why you should go?" she asked.

I shook my head. "Not really, but I see what you mean, kinda."

The gold bracelets on Madame Gerard's arm jingled when she gestured. "Well, make sure to take the ghost with you. I have enough ghosts coming in and out of here. I don't need to add another one."

Sammie and I got up from the table. I motioned for Ama to follow us.

"Thank you again for the information," I said.

Madame Gerard walked us to the door. "Let me know what you find."

I hadn't expected her to say that. I figured she would just be glad to get me out of there and maybe not see me again.

"I'll let you know."

She closed the door and locked it.

CHAPTER 15

*A good display is appealing for customers.
Plus, it might distract them from seeing the
ghosts hanging around.*

Sammie and I headed toward her car. I carried
Van in my arms. Somewhere along the way, I'd
lost Ama. She stood on the sidewalk staring at
Madame Gerard's place. It was almost as if she
was transfixed by the tiny house. Maybe her curiosity was aimed at Madame Gerard. She'd been
awfully quiet while we'd been inside, though
Ama seemed kind of quiet all the time.

I rushed back over. "What's wrong, Ama?"

She didn't acknowledge me for second. But
soon she directed her attention toward me as if
she had suddenly snapped out of her trance.

"Oh, I guess I was just checking out the
place."

That seemed kind of odd, but nonetheless, I
motioned for her to follow us.

"We have to get back. It's getting late."

She got into the car with us, and we pulled

away from Madame Gerard's place. I hated that night had settled around us. And now I had to walk back to the trailer in the dark. Nonetheless, it had to be done. I wouldn't let Sammie walk me back because she would have to go back to her car in the dark. I didn't want to put her in that danger.

Maybe I could call Caleb and have him walk with me. Yes, that was what I would do, even though I liked to think that I could walk back on my own. However, in this situation, it was just too dangerous. And I felt Caleb would agree.

Sammie rolled into the church parking lot as close to the craft fair area as she could get.

"Are you going to walk from here?" she asked with hesitation in her voice.

I knew by her tone that she didn't want me to do that.

I pulled out my phone. "I think I should call Caleb and see if he can meet me here."

"That's a good idea," she said. "I would much rather you do that."

I sent Caleb a text message and hoped that he was somewhere nearby. I didn't want to waste any more of Sammie's time.

"What are you gonna do about what the psychic said?" Sammie asked.

"Well, I guess I have to go to the river and see what she's talking about."

"You're not doing that tonight, are you?"

"No, of course not. I'm not that crazy," I said.

"Whew," Sammie said. "Maybe you should have Caleb go with you there too."

"Yeah, that's a good idea," I said. "I shouldn't

go alone. Though I don't know how I'd convince him that we need to walk down there."

"I think you should do more painting there," Ama said. "If Caleb goes with you, you might not be able to do that."

"I suppose he wouldn't want to hang around while I painted. But I don't want to take the chance of running into anyone dangerous again. Last time, I bumped into Karla. And we all know how she feels about me. She thinks I stole from her."

When my phone dinged, I noticed that Caleb had responded to my message.

I'm at my trailer. How are you?

I'm in the church parking lot, and I'm a little scared to walk to my trailer. I wondered if you could walk with me?

I sent the message. He responded right away.

Of course, I can meet you. I'm on my way.

Sammie gazed up at the black sky with sparkling stars. "Well, it is a perfect night for a romantic walk."

"I hardly think being escorted to my trailer because there's a killer on the loose is romantic," I said.

"You have a point," Sammie said.

Sammie and I sat there discussing lighter topics to take our minds off the heaviness of our recent experiences. We talked about maybe going on a girls' trip soon. Which seemed like a lot of fun to me. I thought a trip to the beach sounded like a great idea.

"We can enjoy piña coladas while relaxing on the sand," I said.

"At night, we can go dancing," Sammie said.

"Oh, that sounds like fun. Can I go too? What's a piña colada?" Ama asked.

My attention shifted to Sammie. "The ghost wants to come with us on the trip."

Sammie's charming, lopsided grin appeared. "Of course, she can come with us."

"A piña colada is a drink," I said. "It tastes like coconut and pineapple."

Sammie laughed at my answer to Ama.

Ama rubbed her stomach. "Sounds delicious."

Movement caught my attention. Still on edge, I jumped and clutched my chest. Thank goodness, it was Caleb approaching the car.

"Oh, he scared me," Sammie said.

"Me too," Ama said.

"Thanks for driving me, Sammie," I said as I reached for the car's door handle.

"You're welcome, Celeste, but just be safe out there. You know I worry about you staying out here with a killer right around the corner," Sammie said.

"Well, it'll all be over soon," I said.

"Don't say that," she said with a frown. "It sounds too final."

"I mean the fair will be over, not that I will be over. At least, I hope not. Call me when you get home," I said as I got out of the car.

"I will," she said.

Ama had already gotten out from the back seat and was beside Caleb. She had slipped right through the car door. Caleb waved as he walked up to me. He tossed his hand up at Sammie too as she drove away.

"Were you ladies out for a late dinner?" he asked.

"Yes, something like that," I said, being a bit vague.

He just quirked an eyebrow but didn't ask for more details.

"Thanks again for coming to walk with me," I said.

"You don't have to thank me for that," he said. "I was more than happy to walk with you. I wish you'd ask me to do this all the time."

"Oh, he likes you," Ama said.

I didn't bother to relay that message to Caleb. No way.

"So at least things have kind of been quiet around here today," I said.

"Yes, thank goodness for that. How are sales going?" he asked.

"It could always be better. I think the murder at the craft fair has slowed things down. To be honest, I'm shocked anyone has showed up. Actually, I can't believe I'm still there. What about you?" I asked.

"It's been pretty good actually," he said. "I'm glad too because I want to use the extra cash to fix up some things around the house. I was thinking that curiosity over the murder has brought more people out."

"That's a bit disturbing," I said.

As Caleb and I made pleasant small talk, I

sensed that someone was watching us. Should I mention this to Caleb or just ignore it? It was probably my imagination. However, when I caught him peering around, I assumed that he had picked up on it as well.

"It seems as if someone is watching us, doesn't it?" I asked.

He took me by the hand. "Yeah, I guess you could say that."

We stopped and peered around at our surroundings.

"I don't see anyone, but they could be hiding anywhere."

Caleb squeezed my hand. "Let's hurry up and get back to the trailer."

We rushed across the field until we made it back to the trailer. I was so exhausted that I was ready to just collapse into bed, but Caleb didn't seem as if he was all that tired.

"Would you like a glass of lemonade?" I asked, trying not to yawn. "We could sit outside and enjoy the breeze."

"I would like that."

After I put Van down for a nap, I grabbed a couple of glasses of lemonade for Caleb and me. I headed back out of the trailer with the glasses balanced in my hands. Caleb met me, taking one. We sat in the lawn chairs in front of the trailer. Lights hung along the outside of the trailer lit up the area with a soft glow. Stars twinkled in the black sky. A warm breeze drifted in from the south.

Caleb and I sat in silence as we sipped on the lemonade. Pierce and I had enjoyed lemonade like this too. I had to admit I'd really enjoyed my time with him as well. How could I have two fabulous guys in my life? Of course, neither one of them had exactly made their intentions known. Sure, I'd had a couple of dates with Caleb, but it wasn't exactly a boyfriend and girlfriend thing. I suppose that was neither here nor there now. My mind was busy solving a murder. We drank our lemonade in silence.

"So are you going to tell me what you all were really doing tonight?" Caleb asked before taking another drink.

How had he known that Sammie and I weren't really out to dinner? Was I that transparent? I supposed I wasn't a good liar.

"What makes you think we weren't out for dinner?" I asked, taking another drink from my glass.

"You always get this expression on your face when you're doing something suspicious. You need to work on your poker face," he said, gesturing toward my face.

I almost spit out my lemonade. "I guess I do need to work on that, right?"

"Just a little bit. So are you going to tell me?" he asked again.

I hated to admit it, but I supposed I had to just tell him the truth. Apparently, he wasn't going to stop asking.

"Sammie and I went to see a psychic. I was

hoping maybe she could help me solve the murder. You know psychics do that all the time."

Caleb focused on me. I was nervous to hear what he had to say about this.

"You're right; they do help quite a bit sometimes. What did she say?" he asked.

My eyes widened. "Really? You don't think I'm ridiculous for doing that?"

"Like I said, they have been known to help. Though I still don't think that you should be involved in the case."

"Well, going to a psychic isn't exactly 'involved.' I was going to relay the information to you."

"So you really didn't find out anything?" he asked with disappointment in his voice.

"No, I suppose I didn't learn anything tonight," I said.

I couldn't help but feel disappointed by that. And I definitely wouldn't tell him that the psychic had told me to go back to the river. He wouldn't stand for that at all. But maybe I should just have him go with me. It would be safer that way. Did I have the nerve to ask him that, though?

"We could always go back to the psychic, and maybe she would have new information. You know, if something came to her, or maybe she will get a vibe off me."

"You really would do that?" I asked.

"Absolutely," he said. "Just let me know when we should go. I'll go with you."

"Yeah, I'd like that."

Since he'd agreed to that, I felt maybe it

would be easier to ask him to go down to the river with me.

"How's your family" he asked. "I really need to get over and see your aunt. I've been craving a burger. How about we go tomorrow?"

"I'd like that," I said.

Caleb and I sat in silence for a few more seconds until I decided to tell him what Madame Gerard had told me.

"Actually, there was something the psychic told me," I said, watching condensation bead up on my glass.

I sensed Caleb staring at me now.

"What's that?" he asked with a raised eyebrow.

"She said I should go back to the river for something."

His eyes widened. "Are you serious? Is she trying to get you killed?"

"She's not trying to kill me. At least, I don't think she's trying to kill me. But apparently she thinks something's there that could help solve the murder."

"The police have been out there so many times. I don't see how they could've missed anything," Caleb said.

"Never say never. It's possible. I mean, things get overlooked. It just happens," I said with a wave of my hand.

"You're not seriously thinking of going there for this item, are you?" he asked. "You don't even know what you're searching for."

"Well, the thought had crossed my mind," I said.

Caleb shook his head. "No way. I think that's a terrible idea."

"That's why I thought maybe you could go with me. I mean, nothing bad can happen to both of us there."

I knew he wanted to say that something could happen, but he didn't want to make me think that he couldn't protect me. I hoped he would see that this was important.

After a few seconds, he released a deep breath. "Okay, I guess we could go there. But you don't think we're going now, right? It's too dark."

"No, of course not," I said with a wave of my hand.

"We could go in the morning when the sun comes up, before everything gets started around here. I'm not sure how I let you talk me into this. I guarantee you, Pierce won't be happy when he finds out about this."

"Yeah, but you want to solve the crime before he does, right?"

He contemplated this thought for a minute, rolling it over in his mind.

"Yes, I suppose that would be nice," he said.

"Besides, Pierce won't know. I won't tell him."

"Okay, but no one knows about this, right?"

I held my hand up. "I won't tell a soul."

He pushed himself up to his feet. "I suppose I should let you get some rest if we're going out early in the morning."

"Yeah, I guess we'd better rest." I fidgeted my hands, unable to hide my anxiety. "Thanks again for agreeing to this."

"I just hope we don't regret it," he said.

"Oh, it'll be fine." I tried to sound confident, although I wasn't sure it was working.

Caleb stood beside my chair now, so I rose to my feet as well. When I took the glass from his hand, our fingers touched. My heart beat faster as he peered into my eyes. His face was only inches away from mine. Was he you going to kiss me? How did I feel about that? I knew if he tried to kiss me, I wouldn't stop him. I would kiss back. Apparently, I wanted it to happen.

He moved closer to my face. His lips were almost touching mine when a loud noise caught our attention. We spun around to see what had happened. I saw no one nearby.

"What was that?" I asked.

"I'm not sure," Caleb said.

"What did it sound like to you?" I asked.

"It almost sounded as if someone was walking this way."

Caleb and I walked to the edge of the trailer and peeked behind it. But again, we saw no one.

"It must have just been the wind blowing a tree branch or something," Caleb said.

"Yeah, I guess that was it," I said, still feeling a bit uneasy.

"Well, I suppose I should get going." Caleb motioned over his shoulder.

"Are you going to be okay to walk to your trailer alone? What if the killer's out there?" I asked.

"I'll be fine. Remember? I'm trained for this kind of thing."

"Oh yeah, right," I said.

"I'll see you in the morning," he said.

Caleb studied every inch of my face for a few seconds before walking away. I tossed up my hand in a wave. He didn't notice.

CHAPTER 16

Secure your displays so that the wind—or ghosts—don't knock them over.

At least the rest of the evening had been uneventful. I had been on edge, wondering if the sound we'd heard was something sinister. That thought had disrupted my sleep quite a bit. But nothing else had happened, so I eventually eased into sleep.

Now, with the morning sun peeking through the blind's slats, I was wide awake. Even though I was tired, I was ready to start the day. Just a bit of sleep had given me revived energy. Now I hoped that my creative juices would flow and I could paint something fantastic today. Plus, I hoped whatever I painted would also contain a message within the images.

Caleb would be here soon, so I had to hurry and dress for our trip down to the river. Still, I wondered if he thought I was a bit loopy for wanting to do this. But bless his heart for not saying anything if he did. After filling up Van's water and food dishes, I headed for my clothing options.

Who was I kidding? There really weren't options. I'd just be wearing a variation of the same thing I wore every day, a T-shirt and jeans. I grabbed a light jacket for my arms because I didn't want any insects or possibly poison ivy to reach me.

"Van, I'll be back soon, okay?" I kissed his cheek and set him back on the floor.

He blinked at me. It was probably just the sunlight in his eyes, but it almost seemed as if he'd winked at me. I headed outside into the warm sunshine. Only a couple of seconds had passed when, glancing to my right, I spotted Caleb walking down the path toward me. He tossed his hand up in a wave. A gorgeous smile came across his face.

"Perfect timing," I said when he approached. "I just stepped out of my trailer."

"Are you ready for this trip?" Caleb asked.

"As ready as I can be, I suppose. Thank you again for going with me."

"I want to—really, I do—so don't worry," he said.

Caleb and I set out toward the wooded path that led to the river. Instead of going on the one that I had taken recently, we headed in the direction of where I had gone originally and found Erica's body. It was the first time I'd gone back down that path since it had happened. My anxiety had increased just thinking about it.

At least Caleb was with me. I wasn't sure I would've been able to go back down this way without him. But Madame Gerard had said I needed to go back to the area, so I supposed she meant the specific spot where Erica had been found.

Caleb led the way as we trailed down the path. The leaves and pine cones crunched under our feet. It was darker under the shade of the trees, and the smell of pine encircled us. With each step closer to the river, my anxiety increased. I had to remind myself to calm down. Flashbacks of finding Erica's body kept coming to my mind.

The sound of the water reached my ears, and the river came into view. We were growing closer. Up ahead was the tree beneath which I had found Erica. Caleb lightly squeezed my hand as if he knew what I had been thinking.

"Are you all right?" he asked.

"I'm fine." I attempted a grin.

I tried to ignore the spot where I'd found Erica, but I wasn't sure how long I would be able to avoid it. We stopped at the river and peered around at the beautiful landscape. I wasn't sure where Ama was this morning. I'd expected her to walk with us.

Madame Gerard had been vague and just said search for something. Well, there was a whole lot of scenery around, and it would be hard to discover anything that was hidden. Caleb and I walked around the area, but there was just absolutely nothing there other than pine cones, branches, and leaves. Nothing that would point to a clue in a murder investigation.

"You know we shouldn't be back here," Caleb said.

"Frankly, I'm surprised that you came. I expected you to tell me that there was absolutely no way you would do this."

"Well, I would've said that, but I had a feeling that you'd do it anyway. And I didn't want that to happen. I think it's too dangerous. I wanted to ask them to close down the entire craft fair."

"Are you serious? I don't think that's necessary, do you?"

"I feel it's better safe than sorry."

I peered out over the water, contemplating Caleb's idea. What he'd said made sense, but I wanted to hang on to the thought that everything would be okay.

"You know I would never forgive myself if something happened to you," Caleb said, breaking into my thoughts.

Just the way he said that sounded romantic. I knew that seemed odd. How could a person be romantic when discussing a murder? But it seemed like more than just a police officer protecting someone. It seemed as if he really liked me. That made butterflies dance in my stomach. I hadn't felt this way in a long time—if ever.

"When I popped up at the trailer and didn't see you, I knew I would find you here," the voice came from over my shoulder.

I jumped a bit and peeked behind me. Ama stood behind us.

"Why didn't you tell me you were coming here?" she asked.

I wasn't sure it was a good idea to talk to Ama with Caleb right there in front of me. She didn't seem to notice that I wasn't talking to her.

She continued. "Did you come here to paint? This is exciting. Now we can really get somewhere." Ama frowned. "But you don't have your canvas or your paints. I suppose you're going back to the trailer to retrieve them."

Yeah, that was it. She really would be upset with me when we got back to the trailer and I didn't gather up my art supplies to go back to the river. I would have to explain to her exactly what had been going on and why I wouldn't be painting there. It would be disappointing for her, but I had my reasons.

"Wait. I know why you came here. You didn't come down here to paint at all. You came down here because Madame Gerard told you to come. I completely forgot about that." Disappointment sounded in her voice.

Now I felt completely guilty. I would have to make it up to her somehow. But how?

"Well, did you at least find anything?" she asked.

"Not really," I whispered.

"What did you say?" Caleb asked.

"I was complaining about the mosquitoes," I said as I smacked my arm, pretending to squish one.

"Oh, they are thick, aren't they? I think I have a million bites on my arm. It was a good idea that you wore that jacket," he said.

"Yes, I thought ahead for once."

"You know, it would be much easier if you just told him I was here and that you are talking to me. He would totally understand," Ama said.

Probably so, but I didn't want to get into it. I just wanted to get out of the spooky setting. Not that the craft area was more comforting. After the murder, a dark cloud had settled over the place. It seemed as if we were all trapped under it. I had a feeling that everyone else felt the same way.

The place didn't have that light and airy feeling, as I had hoped. Ever since the murder, reporters had descended on the craft fair too, making it extremely uncomfortable. A lot of people just wanted to come out for the sake of curiosity. It seemed more like a media frenzy than a quaint craft fair.

I gazed around the area and said, "I suppose this is a pointless trip."

"Well, maybe something else will come to the psychic if we visit her."

"Maybe so," I said, with butterflies in my stomach.

I was glad Caleb was willing to go back to see Madame Gerard with me. Even if it meant nothing new in the case, at least I would have some more time with him. I wanted to get to know him better. Something glimmered under the sun. I stepped over closer to the trees, to the area where I'd found Erica. Being near the spot sent a shiver down my spine.

I spotted a glass bottle on the ground. Picking it up, I examined it and saw that it was an empty bottle of root beer. Someone had just discarded their trash.

"I hate litterbugs," I said, showing Caleb the bottle.

"It doesn't appear as if it's been there long," he said.

"I wonder why the police didn't collect that as evidence? Do you think this trash is evidence?" I asked.

"Most likely not, but you never know." He took it from me. "I'll just give it to the FBI so they can check it out."

"Okay, I guess that's that for this trip." I brushed the dirt off my hands.

I surveyed the area one last time before giving up. I just couldn't understand why Madame Gerard had told me to come back here. The only thing we found was an empty bottle. That didn't seem significant.

Caleb and I headed back down the path toward the craft fair area. My uneasiness waned as I got further away from the area. I never really wanted to go back there anyway, although Ama had wanted me to go there a lot. She wanted me to go back and paint more. I wanted to as well, but I wouldn't go to the crime-scene area. I'd possibly go down to the other side again. It seemed less secluded there. Although I doubted Caleb would want me even to do that, and I wouldn't ask him to sit with me while I painted.

Caleb and I reached the craft area and headed over to my trailer.

"I should get back to work today." He gestured over his shoulder. "I'll see you later for a burger?"

I tossed my hand up in a wave. "I'll see you later."

"I can't wait." His eyes lit up when he spoke.

"Neither can I," I said.

Caleb checked over his shoulder several times as he walked away, I supposed in order to see if I was still watching him. That made him even more adorable to me.

As I set out my paintings, I felt someone watching me. Soon I realized Danny was staring at me. He took a drink from a bottle and went back to his painting. That was when it hit me. What was he drinking? Was it just like the bottle we'd found? My heart rate went up at the thought. I had to see for sure.

I stepped away from my trailer and headed down the path toward Danny's. I tried to keep my eyes off him, but it was almost impossible. Actually, I didn't care if he knew I was staring. After all, he did the same thing to me. He would get a little taste of his own medicine. When I got near the trailer, I knew I had to get a closer look at that bottle. Perhaps I would just come right out and ask him what he was drinking. I could certainly do that. It was not against the law. Weird, maybe, but not illegal.

"May I help you?" he asked in a sarcastic tone. "Is there some reason why you're staring at me?"

"What do you have there? Is it refreshing?"

I groaned internally, knowing how ridiculous I sounded. He scowled, letting me know he thought I was crazy. I didn't care. I just wanted to know what he was drinking. Maybe I would have to wait until he tossed it into the trash. I'd collect the bottle for examination.

"It's root beer," he said in a snotty tone.

I hoped my facial expression didn't give away my shock. This was exactly the type of drink that was in the bottle I'd found at the river. Sure, he could've been there today, but it would be a co-incidence. Other people drank root beer too, but considering I'd bumped into him on the trail that day, I figured this was a huge clue. I wondered if there would be fingerprints on the bottle that we'd found.

"Thanks, I'll have to give that a try," I said.

He gave me another strange glare, letting me know that I should get away. I had no problem leaving his trailer because I didn't want to be around him for a second longer. I had all the info I needed for right now, although I would have liked to get hold of the discarded bottle and possibly get his fingerprints.

Luckily, he had no idea what I was up to, and I wanted to keep it that way. Quickening my step, I headed away from his trailer and back over to mine. I felt his gaze on me as I walked away, but I didn't check to make sure. It would send chills down my spine to see him staring again.

Once back at my trailer, I sat down on the lawn chair and pulled out my phone so that I could text Caleb and let him know what I'd found. My curiosity got to me, and I spied on Danny again. In his usual creepy manner, he watched me.

Focusing on my phone again, I typed out a message to Caleb, but deleted it before hitting SEND. Perhaps I should wait until I actually had the bottle before I told him about this. I could just be jumping to conclusions, and I didn't want him to think I was that impulsive. Although he probably thought that already.

Now I had to come up with a plan to get that bottle out of the trash can. I couldn't just walk up and take it with Danny watching me. Every once in a while, I peered over his way as I painted. He was still sipping the root beer. What was taking him so long? Hurry up and drink it, for heaven's sake.

After about another fifteen minutes, Danny got up and walked over to the trash can. He tossed the bottle toward the container but completely missed. He'd already stepped away at this point, so I assumed he wasn't picking up his trash and placing it in the bin. What a slob. That had been more than he'd done at the river, though. Wait. I was getting ahead of myself. I didn't know that he'd actually left the bottle by the water. That bottle could have absolutely nothing to do with the murder. Plus, any number of people could've left that bottle there.

Nevertheless, I still wanted to get my hands on his discarded trash so that the police could check for fingerprints. If there were prints on the other one and they matched, we'd have found the killer. For all I knew, the cops were already on this, although they hadn't found that bottle. How would I get Danny's bottle without him noticing me poking around?

I supposed I could wait until later when it was dark out. I hated the thought of having to go near him again. There was no telling what he would do if he saw me around. Nevertheless, now I had a late-night mission. At least, it should be a fairly easy one, and I could get it over with quickly, I hoped without being caught or running into Danny.

CHAPTER 17

Remember to have an emergency kit. An emergency can easily catch you off guard. You'll want to be prepared in case you skin your knee, cut your finger, or get a headache from trying to solve a murder.

Later that day, when I stepped out of my trailer, Danny was walking past. This sent a shiver down my spine. I didn't like the idea of him being anywhere near my trailer. Right away, I noticed he was drinking another one of those root beers. He must be obsessed with them. With his stone-cold glare, he soaked in my appearance.

A few seconds went by, and a devilish smile crossed his face. Fear spiked through my body. I couldn't let him know that I was afraid. Thank goodness, he kept walking, though. I watched as he strolled down the path and got into his car. He pulled away, and a breath of relief released from my lips. At least, I felt safer now that he'd gone. He would come back soon enough, though.

"Is he gone?" Ama asked from over my shoulder.

I clutched my chest. "Oh, you scared me."

"Sorry," Ama said.

"Yes, he's gone now," I said. "I think we'll have a bit of time before he comes back, and maybe things will feel safer. He just gives me the creeps." I rubbed my arms as if fighting off the chill he had brought.

"Now that he's gone, maybe you could go back to the river. It wouldn't be so scary. You have to paint more and maybe find clues," she said.

"Do you think clues will come to me? I have serious doubts." I rolled over the thought for a couple of seconds. "Okay, I'll go, but we have to hurry."

Ama clapped her hands. "This is exciting. I wonder what the painting will be this time."

"I guess we'll find out," I said as I grabbed the canvas and my paints.

Van was in the trailer, taking a nap, so I headed out across the way toward the little path that led down to the river. If Caleb saw me, he would stop me in my tracks. Thank goodness, he was nowhere around.

Since the coast seemed clear, I headed down that little pathway with the trees surrounding me. Sunshine broke through the branches, casting a yellow glow around the area. I couldn't imagine coming here at night. It was scary enough during the day. Things grew silent quickly. All the sound from the craft fair was blocked out, by all the trees, I supposed.

I thought the sounds would carry all the way down by the river, but the rushing sound of the water blocked out most of the noise. The only sounds were from birds and insects. I continued down the way until the river came into view. I would sit right there on the bank and do my painting.

Once there, I placed my items out on the ground and sat down by the water. I closed my eyes, trying to collect energy and envision what I wanted to paint. After a few seconds, I opened my eyes, realizing that maybe closing them right now wasn't such a good idea. What if the killer came around? I picked up the brush and dipped it in the green paint. I swiped it across the canvas. Increasingly, the image appeared.

Ama groaned when she saw it.

"What? It's not good?" I asked.

"No, it's not good," she said.

I didn't realize that she was such an art critic.

"I think it's good. He's so lifelike." I pointed.

"It's not your painting. It's the person you're painting," she said. "I don't want him around. Why did you paint him again?"

I raised an eyebrow. "I can't help what I paint. Grandpa seems nice enough. His scowl isn't as noticeable this time."

"Grandpa?" Ama raised an eyebrow.

"I decided I'd call him just Grandpa."

Ama shrugged. "Grandpa should stop popping up in your paintings. He's just trying to irritate me. I had a feeling he would try to poke his way into the living world. He's coming for me."

"Just because I'm painting him doesn't mean

that he'll show up here." I added a few more strokes to the portrait.

"Why not? I did," she said.

She had a point.

"Can you get rid of the painting right away so that he can't come through?" Ama reached for the painting as if she could actually pick it up.

"It's too late for that," a rough, gravelly male voice said.

When I whipped around, I spotted a tall, muscular man standing nearby. He was older, maybe in his seventies, but he was still physically fit. His hair was not even completely gray, and it touched just below his shoulders. He wore the same outfit I had painted before, with feathers in his headband, a fringed tunic, and moccasins. What would I to say to him?

After searching for the right words, I managed to ask, "Who are you?"

As if I didn't already know. To me he was already Grandpa. He appeared exactly the same as I'd painted him on the canvas, with high cheekbones and beautiful, dark brown eyes. A line creased between his eyes, as he hadn't lost his scowl.

"That's my grandfather," Ama said.

Still stunned, I wasn't quite sure I believed that this had happened again. Though it shouldn't have surprised me. I supposed I wanted to ask why he was here, but according to Ama, he had come to get her.

"It's time for us to go back." He motioned for her to follow him.

"I'm not ready to go back. Can't you see I'm

busy? I have things to do here. Now you go away and leave me to it," Ama said, waving her hands.

Uh oh. Anger flashed in his eyes. Obviously, that wasn't the answer he had wanted. I didn't want to be in the middle of this argument. Ama continued shooing him away. He didn't budge.

"You have to come back right now," he said in a booming voice.

Ama crossed her arms in front of her chest. "I'm not going."

Oh no. Maybe I needed to step in and calm them both down.

"Mr. . . . ," I said, not knowing his name. "Your granddaughter is helping me. And I'm sure as soon as she's finished with that, she'll go back."

I smiled, hoping this would ease his anger. But it only seemed to make him worse, as the frown lines on his face deepened. Of course, anxiety spiked through me.

"She doesn't need to help you. What she needs is to come with me," he said.

"I do need to help her," Ama said with a pout.

All right. This wasn't going as I had planned.

"Perhaps we could come to some sort of compromise," I said.

"There is no compromising with him." She pointed.

"Don't talk to your grandfather that way," he said.

There had to be some kind of compromise with these two.

"Perhaps you can tell me why you don't want your granddaughter here," I said.

"This is not where she belongs now. She has to stay with her family on the other side."

"Well, why can't she go back and forth," I said.

The smirk on his face told me that he thought I was either stupid or just naïve.

"Because that causes too much confusion, traveling back and forth between two worlds. What if she gets lost and can't find her way back to us?"

"I don't think that can happen," I said.

"Have you traveled between two worlds?" he asked.

"Well, no, I suppose I haven't," I said.

He looked satisfied that he had proved me wrong.

"I'm not going back, and there's no way you can make me." Ama spun around and headed down the path toward the fair area.

That was when her grandfather took off after her. They left me alone, standing there, confused.

"Hello? Wait a minute." I grabbed my canvas and tote bag full of paint and took off after the ghosts.

They argued as they raced down the path. If anyone saw me running down the path talking, they'd think I was talking to myself. In other words, they would truly think I'd lost it. To their eyes, I would be out here by myself. Was the killer also still out here for me to worry about? And on top of worrying about that, I had to be the referee between two ghosts.

"Will you all wait for me?" I yelled.

It was as if they had forgotten all about me. When we reached the fair area, I wondered if they were going back to my trailer too? They didn't think they'd go inside there and fight, did they?

We spilled out into the craft area. I was right. Ama and her grandfather were headed straight for my trailer. I quickened my step, hoping to block them from going inside. Yeah, right, as if they wouldn't just walk right through me. When I reached my booth, I stood in front of the trailer door.

I placed my hands on my hips. "Stop right there."

Ama and her grandfather stopped moving but continued bickering. Still they paid no attention to me. At least, they didn't go in and scare Van. They stayed right in front me as they continued arguing as if I wasn't even around. Did they do this all the time?

I marched over to them and waved my hand. "Hello? Did you forget about me? Will you all please stop arguing? You are giving me a head-ache."

Of course, they didn't listen. They just kept doing what they obviously did best. Again, I attempted to talk sense into them.

"There has to be a better way than yelling and arguing. Can't we just talk this out?" I tossed my hands up.

"Are you all right, Celeste?" Caleb asked.

I spun around and saw that he was standing there staring at me. I realized that other people were watching too. How easily I'd forgotten that

I was talking to ghosts. Other people were around, and there I was, waving my arms and yelling like a lunatic.

Heat rushed to my cheeks. I knew I had to explain myself to him, but I couldn't even think correctly with their yelling.

I pulled Caleb to the side. "Here's the deal. I have the ghost attached to me, and another one just showed up. They're arguing, and it's giving me a headache."

His eyes widened as he peered over to the spot where I had just pointed.

"Why are they arguing?" he whispered, as if they would somehow hear him.

He didn't know that it wouldn't matter if they had heard him.

"Well, one is the grandfather, and he wants Ama to go back to the spirit world because he doesn't want her away from her family, I guess. He's afraid she'll get stuck here and won't want to go back with him."

"All valid concerns," Caleb said.

Was he mocking me, or did he really believe any of this? Was he just humoring me? For all I knew, he might be thinking of calling for a mental inquest.

"What are you going to do with them?" he asked.

I released a deep breath. "I don't know what I want to do with them. I suppose I just want them to quit arguing, and, well, it would probably be easier if they did move back to their other dimension."

"The grandfather's only here because the grand-daughter's here. So maybe she just needs to go back," Caleb said.

"But she thinks she's here to help me, so until she does, I don't think she's going anywhere."

"Help you with what?" Caleb asked.

"Solving the murder, of course."

He ran his hand through his hair. "I can't believe this. Not only do I have you trying to solve the murder, but now a ghost as well? Everyone wants to be a detective."

"I wouldn't say I want to be a detective, but it's necessary, yes."

"Well, I have to disagree with you on that."

I segued into my next question. "Speaking of the murder, have there been any new developments?"

"Nothing worth mentioning," he said.

I wasn't sure if I believed him. Was Pierce not telling Caleb everything? That was a distinct possibility. It was also possible that the two men were keeping details from me.

Caleb focused on the ghosts again. "Is there anything I can do to help you get rid of the ghosts?"

"I don't think so, but maybe if I took them to the psychic, she would have a way to persuade them to leave."

"That's a good idea. Plus, I said I'd go with you. Maybe we can go after we have that burger," Caleb said.

"I suppose, but we'll have guests along with us."

I raised an eyebrow. "The ghosts?"

"Exactly. I'll just have a talk with them and tell them to calm down until I can resolve this." I released a deep breath as a customer approached. "I guess right now I have work to do, though."

"Good luck, and you know where to find me if you need me." Caleb winked. "I'll check on you soon."

"Thank you," I said.

Maybe Caleb believed me, after all. He seemed concerned and willing to help.

CHAPTER 18

*Stay hydrated. The weather can get to you
and make you feel drained. That leads to not
being able to stay alert and focused. You don't
want to miss a customer—or a ghost.*

By the time the fair had ended for the day, it
was getting late, and I had a headache from the
ghosts' fighting. I spotted Caleb headed toward
me. Gum Shoe walked along beside Caleb. He
had no idea that I'd been listening to the ghosts
all day.

Caleb and Gum Shoe stepped up to the
trailer. "How's it going?"

"About the same," I said.

"They're still fighting?" he asked.

I shook my head. "Yes. I told them if they
don't behave, they're not going out for burgers."

Caleb laughed. "Kind of like kids."

"Yes, actually like children," I said. "Or my
brothers and father."

Caleb laughed again. Putting the dogs inside the trailer, I made sure Gum Shoe and Van had everything they needed before Caleb and I headed toward his truck. I didn't bother to tell the ghosts where I was going, hoping that they wouldn't follow me. No such luck, though. They were right behind us. At least they weren't arguing. They were just pouting.

I had no idea how this would end, because one of these ghosts was just as stubborn as the other. Ama wasn't going back, and her grandfather wouldn't leave without her. I might have the ghosts around for quite some time. As I climbed into the truck with Caleb, the ghosts got on the back. I peered through the back window at them.

"Is everything all right?" Caleb asked.

"They're on the back of the truck," I said.

"Are you serious? I wish I could see them," he said as he started the ignition.

"Be thankful that you can't," I said. "Plus, you don't want to hear them either."

We headed out toward my aunt's diner. It was probably Caleb's favorite place to eat. Which made my aunt happy because, one, she loved the business, but two, she really liked Caleb. Every once in a while, I checked on the ghosts to see what they were doing. More fighting. At least I couldn't hear them from back there. The expressions on their faces said it all.

Caleb whipped the truck into the parking lot. The ghosts bounced around on the back. I supposed they weren't used to automobiles. Caleb found a spot right up front by the door. It wasn't too crowded since it was just after the dinner hour.

Once he shut off the engine, Caleb got out and came around to me. I opened my door first and climbed out, moving toward the back of the truck. The ghosts hadn't even realized that we had stopped. Caleb stood beside me now.

"I think we should just leave them there," I said.

"Good idea," Caleb said.

Inching away from the truck, Caleb and I hurried toward the restaurant, and I hoped that the ghosts wouldn't notice. However, we'd barely gotten to our booth when the ghosts popped up. They stood by the front door, searching for us. A long counter stretched out along the length of the diner, with stools in front where customers could sit and enjoy their food. In the middle was the cash register, and beside that a glass display case of my aunt's best desserts. I had my eye on her famous cherry chocolate cake. I needed to get that recipe from her, but I digress.

After a few seconds, the ghosts spotted us and headed over. Now they were standing behind Caleb. He had no idea. I wasn't about to scoot over so they could sit down. Aunt Patty spotted us and waved a spatula through the air.

As soon as Aunt Patty reached the booth, a line formed between her eyes. "What's going on here? I feel a lot of heavy energy coming from you two. Have you been arguing?"

Her voice dropped as if this would be the worst thing imaginable.

"No, we're not arguing. They are." I pointed behind Caleb.

She scrunched her brow together. "What do you mean? Is someone else with you?"

"Yes, you could say that. We have a couple of ghosts with us."

Her eyes widened. "Do you mean they're haunting the restaurant?"

"Not the restaurant—me," I said.

I'd told my aunt about my recent ghost experiences. Thank goodness, I felt I could tell her anything. The rest of my family thought I was a bit wacky. However, my grandmother and my aunt always understood. Or at least they pretended to understand, even if they didn't. I appreciated that. My mother was too busy taking care of my father and my brothers to even think about anything else.

"Oh," Aunt Patty said through pursed lips. "I guess you can tell me all about that later. Are we in danger?"

"No danger. They're just mad at each other," I said.

"Okay," she said. "The usual for you all?"

"Yes, please," Caleb said.

Aunt Patty walked away, leaving Caleb and me to discuss the ghosts again. I'd rather talk about something else. If only I could block out the chatter from the ghosts. Caleb couldn't hear any of it, so as far as he was concerned, this was a perfectly quiet and charming dinner. But he probably noticed the strain on my face.

"Are they still arguing?" he asked.

"Well, currently they're just standing there, glaring at me. So I suppose I'll have to ignore them for the time being."

"Maybe we should've gone to the psychic first," he said.

"It's okay. I'm sure they'll behave, right?"

A few minutes later, Aunt Patty came back over with the food.

After setting the plates down, she said, "Are they still here?"

I gestured with a tilt of my head. "Right over there. They're being good right now, though. Fingers crossed that continues."

"Well, that's good to know. I'll say a prayer that everything works out," she said, smiling at the location I'd pointed out. "Enjoy the food. I'll talk to you before you leave."

She winked at Caleb again. Surprisingly, the ghosts allowed us to enjoy our food. They were checking out the rest of the restaurant, going around from table to table. People sometimes acted as if they sensed something, but no one had a clue that there were ghosts walking around. It was kind of fun to watch them, actually. When we finished, Caleb and I moved up to the counter to pay for the food.

"Where are you two headed now?" Aunt Patty asked.

"We're going to a psychic," I said.

Her eyes widened. "I suppose that's normal for you. Back in my day, we used to just go see a movie on a date."

This was another date? I supposed it appeared that way, but I was never sure with Caleb.

"Well, we're trying to get the ghosts to move along. Hence the reason for the visit to the psychic." I lowered my voice so that they wouldn't hear.

I didn't want the ghosts to know that was why we were headed to the psychic. If they knew that, they might not want to go inside. I wanted this to go as smoothly as possible. We said goodbye to Aunt Patty and headed outside.

When we reached the truck, we saw that the ghosts had already jumped on the back. They had no idea what I had planned. Caleb pulled the truck out of the parking lot and headed out for the psychic's place, though I hadn't told him where to go.

"How do you know where her place is?" I asked.

"I know where just about everything is in town," he said.

"Yeah, I suppose you would."

I thought maybe he secretly had been to the psychic's place before. After all, he had agreed with the idea of going rather quickly. Maybe he was more open to this kind of thing than he wanted to admit. Soon we had arrived in the parking lot for Madame Gerard's place. Her driveway had been expanded, and the pavement went around to the back of the house. He pulled the truck up and shut off the engine.

"Well, I hope this leads to a successful outcome," Caleb said.

"You and me both," I said as I unbuckled my seat belt.

The ghosts hopped out of the back as Caleb and I got out of the truck.

"Where are we now?" the grandfather asked.

"This is a psychic, and she's going to be able to talk to you as well," I said.

"I don't need to talk to anyone," he said in a rough voice. "I just need for my granddaughter to come to her senses."

"Perhaps that will happen if you talk to the psychic," I said in frustration.

"Doubtful," Ama said in a sassy tone.

As we walked toward the path, I said, "I have to warn you all that Madame Gerard is a bit peculiar."

"Oh, yeah, what does she do that's peculiar?" Caleb asked.

"Well, she has a lot of locks on the door. I'm not sure what that's all about. Plus, she seems a bit suspicious of everyone who comes around, even though she's running a business. I'm sure she'll give you an odd gaze when she sees you."

"I'm used to people thinking I'm a bit peculiar," Caleb said.

"I'm serious. She's an odd duck."

"I wouldn't think much of it," Caleb said. "Duly noted, though."

"I'm not sure that she'll be thrilled to see that I've shown up at her place again. I got the impression last time that she was tired of seeing me."

"How many times have you been in the past?" Caleb asked.

"Not that many, just a couple. But I brought

the ghost around, and Madame Gerard couldn't see her, so I think that upset her."

"So that has everything to do with the psychic and not you," Caleb said.

"I suppose," I said. "At least I hope so."

When we reached the door, I pressed the bell and waited. A couple of seconds went by, but still no sound came from the other side of the door. I peeked over and saw that the OPEN sign was lit up.

"Maybe something's wrong," I said.

"She could be sleeping," Caleb said.

"I don't know, but I am getting a strange feeling. This makes me nervous." I pressed the bell again, just in case she hadn't heard it. "If she's sleeping, maybe the ringing will wake her this time."

Still, after a few more seconds, nothing happened.

"Maybe I'll go around and find a back door. I'll knock back there," Caleb said.

"Okay, I'll stay here."

I watched as Caleb went around the side of the house. If Madame Gerard spotted him back there and didn't know who he was, it would really freak her out. But also, if she was in trouble, I wanted to help. Maybe she had fallen and couldn't get up.

"Is everything all right?" Ama asked.

"I hope so," I said.

"I can go in and see if I can find her," Ama said.

"You shouldn't get involved," her grandfather said.

Before I had a chance to say yes or no or her

grandfather had any other input, she just walked right through the door. He mumbled something under his breath and followed after her. Still there was no sound from the other side of the door. A couple of seconds later, Caleb came back around the side of the house.

"I didn't get an answer back there. The doors are locked, and nothing seems out of place. Maybe she just forgot to flip the sign off and left with someone."

"That's probably the case. At least I hope so, but nevertheless, the ghosts went inside to find her," I said.

"Well, that's a handy little trick, isn't it?" Caleb said.

"I suppose Madame Gerard is used to ghosts coming around anyway, so it shouldn't surprise her if she sees them," I said.

A second later, Ama popped out from the door, along with her grandfather.

"She's inside, and she's tied up with her mouth gagged." Ama rushed the words out.

"Oh, my gosh. Are you serious? Caleb, Madame Gerard is inside tied up."

Caleb pulled out his phone and placed a call. Next, he tried the doorknob.

"No signs of forced entry. The perp might still be in the house with her. I'm going to have to break the door down," he said.

My eyes widened. "You can do that?"

"Well, we'll see," he said.

"I told you she has a bunch of locks on the door. I think they're deadbolts, and breaking those might not be possible."

Caleb backed away from the door a few steps.

"All right, stand back, Celeste," he said. "I'm going to kick it in."

"I wish I could get the locks unfastened. I'd be able to just let you in," Ama said.

That would be fantastic, but I knew it wouldn't happen. I just hoped that Caleb didn't get hurt trying to kick in the door.

"You should stay out of this," the grandfather said.

Caleb ran and kicked his foot against the door where the knob was located. With a loud crash, the door fell to the ground.

My eyes widened.

"Wow, that was impressive," Ama said.

I hoped that Madame Gerard wasn't unhappy that we had knocked her door down. However, we were there to save her. There was no time to be upset about a broken door.

"Stay here, Celeste," Caleb yelled as he ran into the house.

Caleb pulled his gun from his side. Things were getting serious now. I was conflicted about whether I should stay put or not. He had asked me to, but I didn't want him to be in danger while he was in there. What if he needed help?

"Don't worry, Celeste," Ama said. "I don't think anyone else was in the house."

"Oh, good, that means that I can go inside," I said.

"Wait. He told you to stay here," the grandfather said. "Another one who doesn't listen."

I stepped over to the open doorway and peeked inside.

"She's at the back of the house in the kitchen," Ama said.

"Don't encourage her," her grandfather said.

Apprehension took over as I eased into the house. A noise came from the back of the house. Therefore, I had to let go of my fear. *Don't worry, Caleb, I'm here to help.* I hurried the rest of the way into the house. Some of the chairs were knocked over that had been sitting around the table in the living room. Apparently, there had been a struggle.

When I reached the back area, I peeked into the kitchen. Caleb was untying Madame Gerard. Ropes had been wound around her wrists and her ankles. Her mouth had been gagged with a white kitchen towel. Who would do such a thing?

"Madame Gerard, are you all right?" I asked, even though I knew she couldn't answer.

"I told you to stay outside, Celeste. It's dangerous," Caleb said.

"That's exactly why I came in to help," I said. "Ama said that no one else was in the house, so I figured it would be okay."

"Well, you can't take a ghost's word for it," Caleb said.

"You should take my word for it," Ama said with a scowl.

"My granddaughter wouldn't lie," her grandfather said in a growly tone.

Caleb removed the tape covering Madame Gerard's mouth.

"Ouch," Madame Gerard yelled. "Watch what you're doing."

"Who did this to you?" Caleb asked as he proceeded to untie her ankles. "And what exactly happened?"

"I don't know who he was. All I know is he was tall with brown hair. The man just came in here and attacked me."

"Are you physically harmed? Does anything hurt?" Caleb asked.

"I'm all right. He just brought me back here and tied me up. I suppose he was hunting for money. I heard him out there digging around through my stuff. But luckily, I don't keep my money here. There's not much anyway, and I go to the bank often. I know that there are thieves out there, and I'm not gonna let them get to me."

I was just glad that we'd come along when we did. There was no telling how long Madame Gerard would've had to stay in here, tied up, before someone discovered her.

"I had a feeling something was going to happen because this ghost kept coming around, trying to warn me. But I didn't listen. I just kept on doing the same thing I always do, and the next thing I know this person is coming to the door. Why do you think I have so many locks? I don't trust people, and for some reason this guy convinced me that he wanted a reading, and I let him in."

"Well, if the man seemed nice, it's understandable how that would happen," I said. "You didn't know he had bad intentions."

"It's hard to know for sure who is bad. I'm psychic, but not perfect. I can't be expected to sense everything."

"No, of course not," I said.

"Like I said, the ghost was trying to warn me, and next time, I will listen."

"See, this is why you should listen to me," Ama said. "When I give you warnings, you should listen. We ghosts know what we're talking about."

Caleb helped Madame Gerard to her feet.

"What's going on here?" a male voice asked.

When Caleb and I spun around, we spotted Pierce standing in the doorway.

"We found Madame Gerard tied up. Someone broke into her place and attacked her," I said.

Pierce stepped into the kitchen. "Have you checked the rest of the house?"

"It's all clear," Caleb said.

Pierce motioned for other officers to come inside. "See if you can find anything."

The officers rushed inside, fanning out across the house.

"Is this really necessary?" Madame Gerard asked.

"We want to make sure you're safe, ma'am," Pierce said. "We'll dust for fingerprints and any other evidence we can find. Can you describe everything that happened?"

"I have to tell this all over again?" she asked.

When Pierce nodded, she began her story all over again. I listened closely, hoping that she would remember something new this time, but so far, it was exactly the same story. Caleb stood beside me. This didn't go unnoticed by Pierce. Caleb's fidgeting let me know that he felt out of place and unsure of what he should be doing.

He was used to taking over the situation, but now he had to let Pierce handle it.

"It seems like this is just a random burglary," Pierce said.

"I wouldn't be so sure about that," Caleb said. "She could've been followed or otherwise been a target. We've had some break-ins around here lately."

"That's why I said it's probably just a person finding another random target," Pierce said.

Caleb said nothing more, but he still seemed as if he was suspicious of Pierce's answer. I wasn't sure what to think.

"Rest assured, if there's any evidence here, we'll find it. With any luck, we'll get fingerprints and catch the person right away. Everything will be just fine, Madame Gerard," Pierce said.

Based on the frown on her face, I sensed she didn't believe a word Pierce said.

When Pierce stepped away to talk to some of the officers, Caleb went after him. Would they argue? Maybe I should talk to them. Caleb didn't want to be left behind on whatever was happening with the investigation. I walked over to Madame Gerard when the paramedics were finished checking her out.

"Are you sure you're all right now?" I asked.

She waved off my concern. "I will be fine. Don't you worry about me."

Madame Gerard was one tough cookie, and I knew she would be all right physically, but I worried this might have an effect on her mental state. Being attacked was terrifying.

"Don't let them tell you that this isn't connected to that murder," she said with a wave of her slender finger.

My eyes widened. "What you mean? How do you know?"

"It's just a sense, I guess. There's a little voice in the back of my head telling me. I don't know why, but I have a feeling it'll come to me. Just be safe."

I appreciated the warning, but I hoped that Madame Gerard would follow the same advice.

"Are you sure you'll be all right? If you think this is connected to the murder, you should tell the police."

"Do you think they'll listen to me? He already thinks it's a random burglary."

"I can talk to him," I said.

"Like I said, just be careful," Madame Gerard said.

"I promise I will be careful," I said.

"By the way, why were you here?" she asked.

"We came to talk about going out by the river, like you told me. I only found a piece of trash."

"Whatever you found . . . it's significant. I don't care how minuscule you think it is. You must take it seriously."

"I'll take it seriously," I said.

I supposed she could be right about the trash. After all, I had found that Danny drank that same type of soda. So maybe she was right. Pierce and Caleb came back inside the kitchen from the back door. I felt bad leaving Madame Gerard after what had happened, but I couldn't stay forever. She assured me that she would be fine. The police said they would check in on her. After the police wrapped everything up, we said good-bye to Madame Gerard and got into Caleb's truck to head back came to the fair.

"What do you really think happened back there?" I asked when Caleb took off down the street.

"What do you mean?" he asked.

"Do you believe it's a random attack? Because you said otherwise to Pierce."

"I believe it may be that the person had been watching her and knew that she was alone," he said. "Why? Do you think it's someone else?"

"Yes, I do now," I said.

"Like who?" he asked.

"I think that this has to do with the murder at the craft fair."

He flashed a confused expression. "What makes you think that?"

"Because Madame Gerard told me."

"Really? What did she say? Why would she say that?" Caleb stopped at the red light.

I shrugged. "It was just a feeling she had."

"Well, as detectives, we have to go by more than feelings."

"Maybe. But you do have feelings about things, right?" I asked.

"Yes, I suppose that's true," he said.

CHAPTER 19

Secure your displays. A chaotic wind could blow through at any time and spoil all the fun.

Up ahead, I noticed a car pulled over on the side of the road. As we grew closer, I recognized the vehicle and the two men standing outside trying to push the thing. Oh no. Now Caleb eased off the gas pedal and merged onto the side of the road. I knew he would stop. Normally, I would have thought this was a good thing, but considering that I knew the two men trying to push the car, I wasn't sure we should stop. Okay, since they were my brothers, I had to help, but I knew this would end in some sort of catastrophe.

"I'll see if they need some help," Caleb said, shoving the gearshift into PARK.

Obviously, Caleb hadn't recognized my brothers yet.

"You know who that is, right?" I asked.

Caleb shut off the truck. "No, who are they?"

"When you get closer, you're going to recognize them," I said.

Caleb scrunched his brow. "Oh yes, I see who it is now."

He'd tried to sound neutral, but I knew he was a bit worried about the outcome of this situation. Now that we'd stopped, my brothers finally spotted us. Their faces lit up with happiness. They were a pain sometimes, but, of course, I loved them. They really could be sweet most of the time. They just did things that were questionable sometimes, and they acted out before really thinking things through.

Caleb and I got out of the truck and walked toward them.

"What's going on, guys?" I asked.

"Oh, we ran out of gas," Stevie said.

"We were trying to make it to the station, but it didn't happen," Hank said.

"I told him to put gas in the car." Stevie shoved Hank.

"I put gas in the car last time. You were supposed to do it this time," he said, pushing back.

They continued arguing about who had put gas in last.

I clapped my hands. "Guys, guys, don't argue."

"If you want to hop in the back of the truck, I can give you all a ride to the gas station." Caleb gestured.

"Yeah, man, that's great. Thanks a lot." Stevie smacked Caleb on the back.

My brothers climbed into the back of the truck. At least, they knew not to try to put me back there. Caleb and I slid into the truck.

"Thanks for doing this," I said. "I know my brothers can be a bit . . ."

"Quirky?" Caleb finished for me.

"Yeah, that's the word. That word works for the rest of my family too."

Caleb pulled out onto the road. He was laughing now, but that might not continue when he got to know them better. Thank goodness, it wasn't a long drive to the gas station. We had barely rolled to a stop when my brothers jumped out of the back of the truck. I got out and stayed with them as they pumped gas into the container they'd brought. Caleb stood beside me as he watched my brothers.

"So are you guys a couple now?" Stevie asked.

I was afraid this would happen. My brothers were always full of awkward questions. Maybe I should've left them back on the road and made them walk to the gas station. It wasn't that far. They had walked farther. I supposed I just had to deal with their antics now. I knew they were this way, so why had I expected them to behave?

Caleb's expression told me that he didn't know how to answer. And I didn't either. My brothers just laughed when we had nothing to say.

"If you don't want to discuss it right now, that's okay," Hank said. "But you will have to talk about it eventually."

"Don't you have to pay for that gas?" I asked, changing the subject.

"Why? Don't you have the money?"

"Give me the money, and I'll go and pay for

it." I wiggled my fingers. "That way we can hurry and get you back to your car."

"Why? Do you want to get rid of us?" he asked, raising an eyebrow.

"You catch on fast." I waved my hand again to get the cash from him.

"You mean you're seriously not paying?" Stevie asked.

"Very funny," I said.

After reaching into his pocket, he handed me a few crumpled-up bills, and I headed for the store. Should I really leave Caleb alone with them? There was no telling what they would say. I rushed my steps so that I could get back out there before they caused more damage.

When I stepped inside the gas station, a blast of cold from the air conditioning hit me in the face. I went straight to the counter and gave the money to the woman behind the counter. When I spun around, I spotted him. He was at the back of the store by the refrigerator section. Danny was in the gas station.

Panic set in, and I wanted to get out of there right away before he saw me. He was reaching into the refrigerated section for something to drink. More root beer? I had to get away before he noticed me. It was too late. Our eyes met. All I could think about was getting out of there quickly.

I raced toward the door without checking to see if he was following me. Breaking free from the store, I headed toward the truck. My brothers were just putting the gas container on the back of the truck when they noticed me rushing. I ran over to them. Caleb had disappeared. Had they chased him away? It was like ninth-grade prom night all over again.

"What's going on?" Stevie asked. "Are you all right?"

My mind shifted through a bunch of thoughts, wondering exactly how to answer.

"He's in there, and I wanted to get out right away," I said breathlessly.

"Did someone bother you?" Hank asked. "Are you talking about Caleb?"

Anytime they thought someone was bothering me, they were ready to let the guy have it. Needless to say, dating was tough when I was younger. Who was I kidding? Dating was still tough.

"No, it's not Caleb. And the guy in the store isn't really bothering me, I suppose," I said.

"You don't sound convinced about that."

My brothers raised an eyebrow at each other. This was their silent signal to spring into action.

"I think we need to go talk to the guy."

"Where's Caleb?" I asked.

I knew they had probably scared him away.

"He's taking a call and went over there somewhere to hear better with less noise."

I didn't spot him anywhere, but I took their word for it. They'd better not have chased him away. My brothers marched toward the gas station like a two-man army, and I followed them. The last thing I wanted was for them to get into trouble. I didn't know what Danny was capable of, even though there would be two against one. But that *one* was possibly a murderer. My brothers were really like big teddy bears. It wouldn't be a fair fight.

My brothers stepped into the gas station and marched up to the counter. They spotted Danny standing there paying for his root beer. Yes, the same root beer that he had been drinking at the fair. That was no surprise to me.

"Guys, I don't think you should do this. Caleb can talk to him." I grabbed my brothers' arms.

But there was really nothing else for Caleb to say to Danny. He was a murder suspect, and that was all the info we had right now. If looks could kill, Danny would have murdered us all by now.

"Hey, are you causing problems with our sister?" Stevie said, stepping up to the Danny.

"I don't know what you're talking about." Danny grabbed his bottle and headed toward the door.

Hank stopped in front of him. "Just leave her alone."

"I don't know what your problem is," Danny said.

Caleb came into the store. "Is everything all right here?"

"Not really," Stevie said as he stepped closer to Danny.

"All right, guys, break it up." Caleb stepped between the men.

Danny stormed out of the store.

"I told you guys not to say anything to him," I said.

"What? We thought he was bothering you. We didn't want to let him get away with that," Stevie said.

"Guys, we have everything under control," Caleb said.

"Do you really?" Hank asked. "I don't know if you do. My sister's still upset. I don't know if you have it under control."

I waved my hands. "I'm not upset, guys. I just told you who he was, but there's no problem."

"Based on the way you ran out of that store, I'd say there's a problem."

"Did Danny say anything to you before you came out?" Caleb asked.

"No, it's just that same smirk that he always gives, but I'm used to that by now," I said. "All right, let's go, guys."

I opened the door and insisted that they follow me back to the truck. Danny wasn't there. Still on high alert, my brothers climbed into the back of the truck. Thank goodness, nothing else happened as we headed back toward their car.

CHAPTER 20

*Consider giving away small gifts to lure
customers. But don't try giving away your
ghosts. They won't like that.*

A short time later, we arrived back at my brothers' car with no other complications. Danny hadn't appeared anywhere along the way, and my brothers hadn't posed any other questions. Thank goodness, Caleb was nice enough not to mention anything that had happened back at the gas station. He'd ignored the questions from my brothers. I really wanted to ask Caleb about Danny. If he didn't mention him, though, I would have to drop it.

We pulled up to my brothers' car. Caleb and I got out with them, making sure that they filled the tank up and got the car started.

"All right, Celeste and Caleb, so we'll see you all at the festival tomorrow, right?" Stevie asked.

I had hoped they'd forgotten.

"Well, I will be busy with wrapping up the fair. Caleb will be busy too," I said.

"Oh no, you can't get off that easy. You have to hang out with your family," he said.

"We'll see you there," Caleb said.

Stevie and Hank shook Caleb's hand. Apparently, my brothers approved of Caleb and his willingness to hang out with them. Family get-togethers with Caleb? This was a lot more than I expected.

After everything that had happened, I was ready to just go back to the trailer and collapse into that tiny bed. Van would be ready to snuggle up with me too. After saying good-bye to my brothers, Caleb and I got back into the truck.

"Thanks for helping them," I said as he merged onto the road.

"I'm happy to help," Caleb said.

Soon we arrived back at the craft fair. The night sky was full of sparkling stars. Caleb parked close to the trailer so that we wouldn't have a long walk.

As we got out of his truck and headed along toward the trailer, he peered up at the sky. "It's a beautiful evening. Very romantic."

As soon as the words left his lips, my whole body tingled. I'd never heard him mention anything about romance. I didn't know what to think about the comment, but I couldn't help feeling giddy inside. Was he feeling the same way? Was that why he had mentioned the romantic setting? That had to be the reason. Why else would he make such a comment? He was right, though . . . it was romantic.

Well, it was if I ignored the fact that a murderer could be walking nearby. There was hardly anyone out at the craft fair. Everyone had gone to bed for the night, I supposed.

"We really did a lot today," I said around a yawn, trying to make the conversation casual again.

I wasn't sure why I was avoiding any kind of talk of relationship and feelings.

"It's late. I should let you get some sleep," Caleb said.

I supposed he had taken the hint. We walked up to my trailer.

"Well, thanks again for coming with me tonight," I said.

Caleb stood in front of me. As our eyes met, a nervous feeling settled in my stomach again. He moved closer, and I knew what would happen next. He leaned down and kissed me. His lips felt soft as they moved across mine. As we kissed, I had my eyes closed, though almost immediately, I sensed something and opened them. From over Caleb's shoulder, movement caught my attention. Pierce stood at the side of my trailer. He'd definitely seen me kissing Caleb.

Caleb realized something was wrong and moved his lips away from mine. He checked over his shoulder and saw Pierce too. Without saying a word, Pierce walked away. I wasn't sure what to say either. Part of me wanted to run after him and tell him that I didn't know what my feelings were for Caleb. But another part of me didn't want to hurt Caleb's feelings either. Because I liked him.

This dating thing was tough, and I didn't know how it worked. Both guys were nice, and I wasn't sure who I wanted to date. I supposed it would work itself out as I spent more time with the men. I'd spent the most time with Caleb.

"I didn't know anyone was back there," I said.

"I'm sure Pierce was just checking things out," Caleb said.

I could tell he was a bit upset thinking that Pierce had been watching us. As if things couldn't get worse, I spotted a piece of paper taped to the front of my trailer door. I knew right away what it was. It certainly wasn't a notice telling me that I had sold all my paintings, that was for sure. I hurried over and pulled it from the door.

"What is it?" Caleb asked.

"Another warning, apparently." I handed it to him.

You're close, but you'll never be close enough.

After reading it, he said, "This has to stop. I don't think I want you to stay here at the fair anymore."

"I have to stay. I have to sell my artwork. Besides, I think it's just someone messing with me because they realize that I'm poking around the investigation."

"Or maybe the killer is messing with you. Why don't you take me seriously when I say it's dangerous, Celeste?" Caleb asked.

"That isn't exactly a threat," I said. "It's more of a taunt. Besides you're only a couple booths down if anything happens, right?"

"I guess," Caleb said.

CHAPTER 21

Secure your belongings when you have to step away from your booth. Unfortunately, you can't ask a ghost to watch your things. It has to be a person.

Later that night, I needed to grab the bottles of water I'd bought from my truck. I'd only stepped away from my trailer for a short time. I didn't think anything would happen to my paintings and especially in such a short time. I might not be safe from an unknown danger, but I thought my paintings, which I'd left out front before taking them in for the night, would be fine. I was completely wrong.

When I reached my trailer, I stopped in my tracks. It felt as if someone had punched me in my stomach. I was unable to breathe for a second, as if the air had been sucked out of my lungs. I thought I might be sick right there.

The slashed canvases took my breath away. In the middle of several of my paintings, the canvas had been cut. Who would do such a thing? Peering around for the culprit, I saw no one else out at their trailers. However, I had a feeling the person was close by. Someone obviously didn't like me and was trying to send a message. Perhaps the same person who had left the notes. It wasn't just a random person who had come along and stumbled on my paintings, deciding to destroy my hard work.

I suspected either Danny or Karla. And I intended to get to the bottom of this. They wouldn't get by with doing this to my artwork. Who should I confront first? Now I was angry. At first, I'd been scared, but now anger had taken over.

I walked toward Karla's place. Maybe Danny had really done it, though. Either way, I was going to confront someone. I knew whoever did it wouldn't want to admit their guilt, but at least if I knew who it was, I'd be aware of their violent nature in the future. And I wouldn't let them get away with what they'd already done.

Of course, if the person who'd done this was the killer, they'd already showed their nature toward Erica. What was I supposed to do? Allow this to happen without saying a word? No way. That wasn't my style.

The light was on at Karla's trailer. I intended to knock on the door and ask her about slashing the paintings. Of course, I was anxious as I approached the door. I reached up and pounded on it. It was now or never. I would just have to come right out with it.

Now that I had knocked, second thoughts crept into my mind. Should I really do this?

When Karla opened the door wide, I knew that I had no choice but to go through with it. Anger filled her expression as soon as she saw me.

"What do you want?" she yelled.

"I want to know why you destroyed my paintings," I said.

When I threw the anger right back at her, I hadn't expected such rage to fill her eyes.

"Exactly what are you talking about? I know you're not accusing me of something like that."

I stood my ground. "Yes, I am accusing you. I know you're angry with me for confronting you with Erica's murder. And you think I stole your wallet. So that's the perfect excuse for you to try to get revenge against me. Someone destroyed my paintings, and I know it was you."

Rage filled her eyes, and I thought she might jump right out of her trailer and attack me.

"Maybe you shouldn't leave your things out where people can destroy them."

"So you're admitting it?"

"I'm not admitting to anything," she said.

"Stay away from my things," I said.

"What makes you so sure that it was me? Maybe it was one of your other neighbors? Like that creepy guy on the other side with those horrific paintings. It could be your boyfriend the cop. Did you make him mad? I saw the other one lurking around. If you're going to point fingers, definitely do it at them and not me."

"I'm sure you just want me to think it's the crazy guy. That would be the obvious choice. And don't even think it's one of my friends."

"You're such a fake. You go around trying to be all nice, but I know that we should really watch you. You try to be a sweet little girl, driving that pink truck and the pink trailer. You're trying to act like you're innocent. Well, I'm not buying that act. How do I know you didn't slash your own paintings so that you could accuse me of doing it?"

"I've heard a lot of crazy things, but that's the craziest," I said.

There was no sense in talking with her any longer. I spun around and headed back toward my trailer.

"What's going on here?" Caleb called out.

Thank goodness, Caleb was there.

"Look what she did to my paintings," I said, pointing.

"Don't accuse me of that." Karla lunged toward me. Caleb jumped in front of her.

"Celeste, go back to the trailer, and I'll be right there, okay?" Caleb held Karla back with his arm.

After giving one last glare, I marched the rest of the way over to my trailer. I was so upset that I wanted to scream. Many of the paintings were ruined. I had very little left to sell now. Even if the craft fair was almost over, it still meant potentially less profit for me. There would be no time to replace them. Plus, I'd lost all the hard work that had gone into the paintings.

What made her think she had a right to destroy them? And what was her reasoning? Other than just being angry with me. I supposed I still could possibly blame Danny for it. I just got the feeling that Karla had been the perpetrator. From the second she'd stepped out of her trailer, I'd sensed her guilt. It was almost as if she had been waiting for me to discover what had happened.

I stood in front of the paintings and tried to force back the tears. Forcing myself to keep it together, I stood tall to show her that I wouldn't let this get to me. I would just have to make do with the paintings I had left. Sure, it was a setback, but I wouldn't let that stop me.

Out of curiosity, I held a glass jar up to one of the paintings. That was odd, I thought. I stepped over to another one. The same thing had happened. Oddly enough, Karla had stabbed right into the hidden images in the paintings. If anyone ever saw me holding a glass up to the paintings, they would think that I'd lost my mind. I'd just tell them it was my unique way of painting. It was just a way for me to see the work that I'd done. That was the truth, in a way. If I wanted to see what images I'd painted, it was the only way.

I focused my attention on Karla's trailer now. Caleb still stood next to Karla. With her arms crossed in front of her, she nodded at what he said. After a few more seconds, Caleb came back over to me.

"Are you okay?" He touched my arms.

"Yeah, I guess I'll be fine. It was just a shock to see." I pointed.

He studied the paintings. "I'm really sorry this happened, Celeste."

"I only stepped away for just a couple minutes. I never dreamed anyone would do something like this. What did she say?"

"She denies that she had anything to do with it. You'd have to get some kind of proof."

"Well, I don't have anything like that. There's no video or pictures. But I'm beginning to think that maybe I should have some kind of surveillance."

"It might not be a bad idea," he said.

I had hoped he would say that it wasn't necessary. But unfortunately, I knew it probably was needed.

"I'll help you put this away if you'd like."

"At least I can salvage the frames," I said.

"That's thinking on the positive side," he said.

"I have nothing else, so I have to keep positive. I just want to make sure she stays away from me," I said.

"Thankfully the fair is almost over."

"Maybe I'll never see her again. But what if she's a murderer? She'll be getting away with it."

"I can guarantee you were not going to let this killer get away with it." Caleb sounded angry.

Caleb helped me lift the damaged canvases into my little storage spot in the trailer.

"Now I have to paint new paintings. But, unfortunately, there's no time before the fair opens again in the morning. I'll just have to put out what I have."

"What makes you think Karla did this?" Caleb asked.

He sounded as if he really didn't want to ask,

but I knew he had to try to get the facts. I explained to him that she had been watching me.

"I know that's not definitive proof. I'll just have to say that I'm suspicious," I said.

"I'll keep my eye on her. If I find out she did this, we can arrest her."

"Thank you, Caleb." I stood at the trailer door. "I should get inside and feed Van."

"Yes, I'm sure Gum Shoe is waiting for me too." He studied my face. "Make sure your door is locked."

I knew this place was dangerous, but to hear his warning sent a shiver down my spine. Caleb touched my hand and gave me a lingering kiss. He waited while I closed the door. I figured he was listening to hear the lock.

A short time later, I was all cuddled up in bed with Van beside me when the doorknob rattled. Van barked, and I sat up in bed. My heart sped up. The sound had stopped, but that did little to ease my fears. Now I had to get up and see who was at the door. Of course, there was no way I would open it.

The tiny window on the door would allow a glimpse of who might be on the other side. However, the small window on the side of the trailer would probably offer a better view. Yes, peeking out the window on the side would be better than the door. I just didn't want to be greeted with a face if I peered out the door window.

I picked up Van. He was now growling, which he didn't do often. That scared me even more. Whoever was on the other side of that door probably wasn't here with the best intentions. Especially at this time of night. Could it be Caleb or Pierce? I thought for sure they would say something and let me know if they were here. They wouldn't want to scare me this way.

I stood beside the small window, holding Van in one arm and lifting the slat of the blinds with my other hand. My hand shook so badly that the blinds moved too. Now I worried that the person at the door would see the movement. I'd wanted to be a bit more undercover and go unnoticed.

Peering out the window, it was hard to make out much in the darkness outside. But as far as I could tell, there was no one at the door. Ama wasn't capable of rattling the doorknob. Plus, she would just pop up in the trailer and make herself known. Grandpa too. I had a terrible sinking feeling that someone wanted to get into my trailer. There was no way I was going let that happen if I could stop them.

As best as I could, I scanned around the entire area. I saw nothing out of the ordinary. There were no people out at this time of night. Everything was locked down. I'd seen a couple of police officers earlier patrolling the fair. I assumed they were walking around the area now, but I knew they wouldn't try my doorknob without announcing that they were here.

My nerves had settled down somewhat, but I was still on edge. There was nothing I could do, I supposed, so I just settled back down under the covers with Van. I wasn't sure I would be able to go back to sleep now. I closed my eyes and tried, because I knew I had to get up soon and get to work. Should I try counting sheep? I doubted that would work. Van didn't have any problem going back to sleep, though. At least I had him next to me, and I knew that when he got the slightest sense of someone coming around, he would jump to attention.

Drowsiness had just taken over when the door rattled again. My heart sped up so fast that I thought it might pop right out of my chest. Of course, Van barked again and growled. I picked him up and repeated the same routine as earlier, going to the window and checking to see who was there.

I had a feeling someone might just be playing tricks on me since I saw no one. There was no way to be sure, though. I couldn't go outside the trailer to check. What if the killer was the one playing tricks and trying to lure me outside? I'd just stay put until daylight.

Maybe I should text Caleb or Pierce and let them know what was happening. Again, what if it was really nothing? I always worried that I might disturb them for nothing. If someone was just playing tricks, it was pointless to let them know. Although playing tricks with still kind of serious when a killer was around.

CHAPTER 22

*Bring snacks to keep up your energy as you
sell your crafts, get to know other vendors,
and solve a murder.*

The next morning, I decided I needed to go to
the bakery again and try to speak with April. I
wasn't sure if I would find out anything new, but I
had to give it a shot. Things were getting bad
quickly, and the craft fair was almost over. I would
have to figure this out before something else happened—like someone else getting killed . . .
namely me.

After getting dressed, I skipped breakfast,
since I could get something at the bakery. I'd be
there and everything, so I might as well treat myself. Van would have to stay at home since they
wouldn't allow him in the bakery.

"I promise I'll be back soon, Van," I said.
"Maybe I'll bring you a special treat from the
doggie bakery."

The pet store was down the street from the

bakery. I'd have to stop for a quick trip on my way back. Van wagged his tail and licked my cheek as I hugged and kissed him good-bye.

When I stepped out of the trailer, I checked to the left and to the right, making sure Danny or any other of the suspects weren't around. No one seemed to be near. I hurried to the truck so that I could get out of there before someone showed up. Caleb wasn't out at his booth either, which was probably for the best. The last thing I needed was for him to figure out what I was up to.

After slipping behind the wheel of my truck, I headed down the road to the bakery. For the entire drive, my mind was occupied with trying to solve the murder. Why couldn't I narrow this down more?

Thank goodness, I found a spot right out front. I'd assumed the bakery would be busy this time of morning. Once I'd parked, I got out of truck, locked it, and headed for the door. Of course, I scanned my surroundings to see if anyone had followed me this time. Thank goodness, I saw nothing out of the ordinary. I was on high alert for something to happen. Someone could've easily followed me, and I wouldn't even know.

When I stepped inside the shop, I was surprised to see that there really weren't that many people there after all. Just a few customers stood at the counter. The same woman who had helped me before was working today. Disappointment settled in. I had hoped to find April here. When did she work? Now I'd just have to

make a purchase and ask the woman if there
were any new updates. At least I'd have breakfast
now.

The smell was delicious inside this place.
What would I order? A donut? A pastry? Maybe a
croissant? There were so many options. After all
the stress, I deserved a treat. I'd been good with
my healthy eating, and it was time for something
special. No one had noticed that I'd entered the
place. I stepped up to the line at the counter to
wait. Leaning to the left, I tried to get a glimpse
of the contents in the glass containers.

A couple of minutes later, the woman had
helped the other customers, and I was next. Before she had a chance to take my order, April
came out from the back. Holding back my excitement was tough. I almost yelled out with
glee. Now maybe I'd get a chance to talk to her
after all. I just hoped that she didn't go back
through that door without giving me a chance
to talk to her first. How would I explain that I
needed to speak to her? It had to be subtle.

When our eyes met, she instantly recognized
me. April frowned at first, as if wondering why I
was there. However, a couple of seconds later, I
supposed she realized that this was a business
and that I was here for food. She didn't need to
know that it was more than that. Although when
I asked questions, she might be suspicious. Still,
the expression on her face wasn't friendly. I'd
done nothing wrong, so I wasn't sure why she re-
acted that way.

"May I help you?" she asked in an unpleasant
tone.

I still hadn't decided what I wanted to purchase, but I knew I needed to make that decision quickly before April told me to get lost.

"I'll have a glazed doughnut, please," I said.

She said nothing as she picked up one of the doughnuts from the glass case and placed it into a bag.

"That'll be two dollars, please." She thrust her hand toward me, waiting for me to hand over my dollar bills.

I had no idea what to ask her, and it seemed as if I'd have to leave without asking any questions at all. Once she had my cash, she walked over to the register to place the money inside. I supposed it was time for me to leave. She was distracted with trying to get the register to work. Right there on top of the counter, April had left her phone for anyone to see. Maybe I could just take a quick peek. After all, she was distracted. It was practically an invitation to sneak a peek.

If April caught me, she would probably come right over the counter and attack me. I had no idea if she was the killer or not, so should I really test her patience? She could be capable of something horrific. I didn't want to think that about her, but I had no choice. Also, I had no choice but to check the phone. It had to be done. I leaned over and touched the phone's screen. Immediately, it lit up.

Everyone was busy and paying no attention to me either. What was I even expecting to find on the phone? I'd better figure it out soon. My heart beat quickly. Was I actually doing this? Thank goodness, Pierce and Caleb couldn't see me.

The easiest thing for me to check was the text messages. I clicked on the little icon. Text messages from Mark showed on the screen. However, before checking out the messages from him, I saw an exchange between Erica and April. She still had that on her phone? I supposed it had only been a few days. If I had lost Sammie, that would have been a grim reminder. I wouldn't be able to handle that.

Erica and April had communicated not long before Erica's murder. It was tough to read the text while the phone was upside down, but the last thing I wanted was to touch the phone in case April noticed me. I was running out of time.

The text message exchange was that April knew about Erica's secret hiding place. What was that supposed to mean? Erica had a secret hiding place? What was it for, and why was it secret? Even stranger was that April had wanted Erica to meet her at the secret hiding place right before the time when Erica was murdered. That sent a chill down my spine.

CHAPTER 23

Make sure to give a receipt. Accept a credit card if you can. Keep records of your customers. You never know if you may have to call them as witnesses.

Thank goodness, I'd stopped invading April's privacy seconds before she spun around. She frowned, though, as if she was suspicious of me. She noticed her phone on the counter. For a second, I wondered if she knew I'd been checking it out. She was a sharp cookie and intuitive, obviously. Did they have a video camera in this place? April might go back and check the video to see if I had been up to something. At least I would be out of here by then. But she might come after me, especially if she was the killer. I had just put myself in an even riskier situation.

"Did you need anything else?" she asked in a snippy tone.

"Do you remember me? I spoke with you at the craft fair. Remember? You came by asking questions about Erica," I said.

She raised an eyebrow. "Yes, I remember you."

"How are you doing?" I asked.

"As well as can be expected, I suppose, since my friend was murdered."

"Have the police talked to you about any clues? I know that you were trying to get some on your own," I said.

She still seemed hostile and tense. "No, I have no new clues. I suppose it's just a closed case now."

"I wouldn't give up on that just yet," I said. "Do you know where Erica was going right before she was murdered? Did she have someplace she had to be?"

"Why are you asking these questions?" April asked.

"It just crossed my mind that perhaps asking you questions would help you remember something about a clue or refresh your memory."

More customers came in. "I don't have any more information, and I have to go back to work."

She moved away from me and over to a customer.

I headed outside with my doughnut and climbed back into the truck. As I sat inside the truck, I devoured the doughnut. It was more of a pity treat since I hadn't come up with any new clues, and it seemed as if I wasn't any closer to solving this crime.

With glaze icing on my lips, I peered around to see if there was any suspicious activity. Thank goodness, I saw nothing out of the ordinary. I remembered what the woman at the fair had told me very early on after Erica's murder. Erica had worked at the school as the art teacher. Maybe I needed to go by there and see if anyone would speak with me about Erica. Maybe they would have information that they'd recently remembered or forgotten to share with the police.

After finishing off the doughnut, I started the truck and backed out of the parking space and headed for the school. Classes would be starting soon, so I would have to hurry or else I would have to wait until the end of the day. Luckily, I had gone out early, or none of this would've been possible.

A short time later, I pulled into the school's front circular drive. In a landscaped area in front of the school, there was a tall pole, and an American flag waved proudly in the wind. To the left of the school was the parking lot. I made my way around to that parking lot and found a spot. The traffic from parents dropping off students was just clearing out.

As I hurried out of the truck, I realized the adults were headed inside. The students were already there. Only a few people lingered around, and I assumed they were heading in too. I made eye contact with one woman and hurried over to her. She was trying to avoid me, but it was too late.

I was close enough now to say, "Excuse me."

She eyed me up and down, and said, "May I help you? If you need to speak with a teacher, you'll have to check in at the office."

"Actually, I just have a quick question, if you don't mind. I'm investigating the murder of Erica Miller. Did you know her?" I asked.

She peeked around as if she was making sure no one was watching. Why would she be worried that someone would hear us talking?

"It's just awful what happened to her, and I hope they find out who did this soon. We're all worried and scared. What kind of questions do you have?" she asked.

"Just anything that you can tell me about her," I said

"Erica was very sweet person. And trusting, probably to a fault. I feel like maybe that's what got her into this situation."

"What do you mean?" I asked.

"Well, maybe someone like the killer asked her for help or whatever, and they lured her into that area."

"You don't think she was there on purpose and the killer just found her there? Like a random attack or something?"

"I don't think this was random at all. I don't know, I guess; it's just a gut feeling," she said.

"Do you have any idea who may have wanted to harm her?" I asked.

"No. As far as I know, she wasn't dating anyone, and she spent most of her time working with the art materials and preparing for her class here. I don't think anyone had any issues with her." She checked over her shoulder, and I knew she had to leave.

"All right, thank you for the information," I said.

"You're welcome," she said.

"Oh, one more thing before you go. Do you know anything about a secret meeting place?"

She tapped her index finger against her bottom lip, trying to think of something. "Wait, there is one thing that could possibly be it."

Excitement settled in as I waited for her response.

"She talked about going down to the river to paint. But that was some time ago. I don't know if she still did that. Maybe that could be the secret meeting place, as you called it."

Perhaps she was onto something with that. If she called it her secret hiding place, that would make sense.

"Thank you again for the information," I said.

"You're welcome, and I hope you find out who did this. What was your name again?"

"Celeste Cabot," I said.

"I haven't spoken with the officers in a few days, but I was hoping they'd made progress."

She had no idea that I wasn't with the police department. I certainly couldn't tell her otherwise.

I waved. "Good-bye."

Pierce was currently texting my phone and telling me that he needed to speak with me. Was I in some kind of trouble? Did he know I was here? I scanned the area for any sign of him. As soon as I got back to the truck, I'd have to call him. Needless to say, I was a bit nervous to hear what he had wanted.

Once in the truck, I placed the call, but it went to his voice mail. Maybe it wasn't that important after all. Perhaps he was just calling to see if I wanted to have lunch. The thought made me happy and nervous at the same time. I supposed I could say yes to lunch. However, I couldn't take him to my aunt's place. It would be too awkward for her to see me there without Caleb. She'd automatically think that I was cheating on him.

I sent a text message and let Pierce know that I had received his message and had tried to call him back. As I shifted the truck into gear, I noticed something kind of unusual.

Someone was sitting in a car nearby. I thought she had been watching me. However, I couldn't say for sure because she had on sunglasses and a hat. She diverted her attention from me. Perhaps she'd just been watching me for innocent reasons, which was nothing unusual. That happened every day, but I just had a bad feeling about her sitting there with that huge hat and sunglasses as if she was trying to be incognito.

Had she really been watching me on purpose, with more sinister intentions? Or was it completely innocent? I wasn't sure what to do next. What if I left and she actually followed me? I supposed that was a chance I would have to take. I couldn't sit in the parking lot all day.

After sitting there a couple more minutes and not hearing from Pierce, I decided that I had to leave. After shifting the truck into DRIVE, I headed out of the parking lot. As I pulled out onto the street, she didn't even acknowledge me. That was a relief.

It had just been my imagination. I was being

too worried about every little thing. Which was totally understandable, considering there had been a murder, but I couldn't let that control my every thought. And I certainly wouldn't live in fear because that was what I said I wouldn't do—live in fear. Now I was doing exactly that. I flipped on the radio and tried to let the music distract me as I cruised down the road, headed back toward the craft fair.

As I cruised through the next green light, I realized that the woman was following me. Well, I supposed I couldn't say for sure. Maybe it was just another coincidence that she was behind me. But in light of recent events, I had to keep my eye on her. What if she followed me all the way back to the craft fair?

What could I do to find out if she was really following me? It wasn't like I was going to stop and walk back to her car and ask her. She could be a deranged lunatic, for all I knew. I would try to put some distance between us and, with any luck, get away from her. Thank goodness, the next light changed to green and didn't stop me. I didn't want to take the chance of having her sitting right behind me at the light.

Up ahead, I made the next right instead of waiting and going two streets down to head back to the craft fair. I wanted to see if she would follow me this way. The next street just led to businesses that I knew were closed for a few more hours. So she probably wouldn't have any reason to go this way unless she was truly following me.

My anxiety ramped up as I drove. After traveling a bit down the road, I saw that she was still following me. This wasn't good. What would I do now? How would I get away from her? I supposed the next street to the left would lead me back over to the road that led to the craft fair. I would have to take that and try to get away from her that way. I was just stunned that she was actually following me.

The woman stayed with me the entire time that I drove to the next street. She followed me all the way to the craft fair. I was completely panicked. To make matters worse, I couldn't stop driving long enough to text Pierce or Caleb because I couldn't take my eyes or hands off the wheel. This was a dangerous situation.

Perhaps if I got to the craft fair and she was still following me, I would be able to alert someone to the situation. What did this woman want? Why was she following me? Thank goodness, the church came into view up ahead. I whipped the truck into the parking lot, trying to keep my focus on driving, but also looking in the rearview mirror to see if she was still following me.

To my relief, the woman continued down the road and didn't pull into the church parking lot. What was that all about? Surely, she had been following me. There was no way that she'd kept up with me for that long and it wasn't on purpose. She just didn't want to follow me all the way into the church parking lot. She knew who I was and why I was here. Now I just had to find out who she was and what she wanted.

Thank goodness, she hadn't followed me here, but she would probably be back. No doubt, we would meet again. I pulled all the way to the back area of the lot. After parking the truck, I got out and headed toward my trailer. I hurried around the side of my trailer, keeping my eyes open for any sign of something strange.

As far as I knew, Caleb wasn't at his trailer. I wasn't sure if I should text Pierce or Caleb after all. Perhaps I would just keep my eyes open for her. If it happened again, I would definitely tell them. In the back of my mind, I knew that she had followed me on purpose. I just wanted to have proof before I said anything.

The itch to paint came over me. Was it because a message was trying to come through to me? Just as I thought about collecting my supplies to paint, the sound of traffic came from nearby. Stepping around to the other side of the trailer, I spotted the crowd gathering in the distance. I'd totally forgotten about today's events.

CHAPTER 24

During the slow times, check out other places and things at the craft fair. Compare prices. Get ideas. Look for ghosts and murder suspects.

The fact that today was the annual craft fair closing party had slipped my mind. Everyone was flocking to the large field area behind the church for food, fun, and games. There would be hamburgers, corn dogs, cotton candy, caramel apples, funnel cakes, and fried everything. I spotted the clowns across the way. They were already making balloon animals for the kids. There were even pony rides.

I knew my family would make an appearance soon. And if they caught up to me, I would never be able to paint a new hidden message. I definitely didn't want my brothers' input on my art. That would be a disaster for sure.

"What are you doing?" Ama asked.

I jumped again. "Oh, you scared me."

"Sorry," she said sheepishly.

"What are we doing now?" Grandpa scowled.

"I'm scanning the crowd for my family. I don't know what to do with them if they show up."

"You don't want to see your family?" Grandpa asked.

"Not right now," I said.

"That's disgraceful," he said.

"If you met my family, you would understand."

"That's true, Grandpa. I've met them, and they are definitely different."

He shook his head. "No matter. Family is family. If they're on their way, you should stay here and wait for them."

Without listening to his advice, I decided to leave. I'd only moved an inch when I spotted my brothers. Unfortunately, we made eye contact. It was too late. They'd seen me. I waved as they walked toward me.

"What should I do now?" I asked.

"I guess you have no choice but to stay with them. Oh, I know, just tell them there's a few things you have to wrap up. I bet they'll understand," Ama said.

"You stay out of this," Grandpa said.

"Oh, here come my mom and dad now."

"See, it's good that you stayed," Grandpa said.

"Just wait until you meet everyone," Ama said.

"They can't be that bad."

My brothers approached first.

"What's going on, sis?"

I gestured over my shoulder. "I was just going to wrap things up at the trailer so we can enjoy this day."

"You mean you haven't finished everything

yet? You knew we were coming. You should've had all that done."

I had a murder investigation to wrap up. That was what I had to get done.

"I entered the hot dog eating contest." Stevie pointed out the sign.

Oh no. This wouldn't end well.

"I don't think you should try that," I said.

"Are you kidding me? I can eat more hot dogs than anybody here," he said.

"But you can't eat more than me," Hank said.

I faced Ama. "See, this is why I said this was a bad idea."

I'd forgotten and talked to Ama.

"Who are you talking to? Are you completely insane?" Stevie asked.

"All right, if you must know, there's a ghost here."

They burst out in laughter. Which was exactly what I knew they would do.

"I'm being serious, you guys. Plus, there's another ghost right there." I pointed at Grandpa.

"You really are a wacko."

Why did I feel like I was twelve again?

"Okay, fine, don't believe me," I said.

"I should do something to make them believe you," Ama said. "I don't know what, but surely I can do something."

"We can just get out of here, that's what we can do," Grandpa said.

"I have to do something so that they know that Celeste is telling the truth." Ama waved her hand in front of their faces.

They didn't notice a thing.

"Are you going to watch us eat the hot dogs?" Hank asked.

"Fine, I'll do it," I said.

I was just stalling for time anyway until I could reach Caleb or Pierce. I walked over with my brothers to the table where they were setting up for the hot dog eating contest. Grandpa and Ama came with us.

"Why are they doing this?" Grandpa asked.

"I guess just to impress everyone with their abilities and win money," I said.

Grandpa shook his head. "Those are crazy reasons."

Stevie and Hank sat down at the long table full of hot dogs, taking their positions to start the contest. Soon the timer went off, and the contest was underway. I had to admit they were in the lead. They were basically competing with each other.

I scanned through the crowd to see if I recognized any familiar faces. I thought for sure I'd seen someone watching us from a distance behind one of the trees. The person wore a large straw hat and dark sunglasses so that I couldn't make out who it was, but I thought for sure they had their eyes set on me. That sent a shiver down my spine.

When the person realized that I had noticed them, they moved behind a tree again. Naturally, I was curious as to who was watching me. But I also wasn't sure that I wanted to know. What if it was the killer? I wished I could get a better view. With everyone distracted by the contest, I decided I would get a bit closer. Not too close. I didn't want to get away from the crowd. Heading toward the trees, I stepped away from the main fair area.

"Where are you going?" Ama asked.

"Someone was watching us from behind that tree over there," I said out of the corner of my mouth.

"That's where you're headed now?" Grandpa asked. "That's a bad idea. It could be dangerous."

"I'm not going too close," I said.

I weaved around two people eating cotton candy and a couple of clowns who tried to make me laugh with their dancing. They were giving me anxiety. Maybe not a full-on panic attack, but their dancing was still panic-inducing. I made my way around them and decided that I was now close enough. But I saw no sign of the person who had been watching me.

The person must have taken off when they saw me headed that way. And that was probably a good thing. I didn't want to encounter the killer. However, I wanted to find him so that we could put him in jail. My attention went back over to the crowd to see what was going on with the hot dog eating contest. Surely, they'd be done soon.

CHAPTER 25

*Don't back out and leave the fair before it
ends. You might miss out on late customers—
or the chance to solve a murder.*

Out of the corner of my eye, I caught movement. On my left, I spotted my neighbor. Karla
didn't acknowledge me. That was probably just
as well since we weren't exactly on friendly
terms. I had given up hope of her being friendly.
Regardless, she was still on my list of suspects
anyway. And she would remain there until I had
reason to take her off. More than anything, I
wanted to find a reason to take her off. I wanted
to narrow down the list more than anyone.

On the table next to her craftwork, I noticed
something. A pair of sunglasses. Of course, lots
of people had sunglasses, so that wasn't unusual,
but they were a lot like the pair I'd seen the
woman in the car wearing. Maybe I was jumping
to conclusions, because I hadn't been able to
see her well. All I knew was that they were big,

black, and round, like the sunglasses on Karla's table.

But still that was in my mind now. Finding out that she was the killer wouldn't be out of the realm of possibility. After all, she was on my list. Maybe she was the killer and felt I was getting too close to solving this crime. It could have been her in the car. All that was missing was the hat. Perhaps I would see that nearby. Was Karla the person in the vehicle? I had no idea what kind of car she drove. She wouldn't follow me in her car, would she?

I had to find out what kind of car she drove. Karla got up from her chair. Now was my chance. I had to follow her. I trailed her down the path toward the parking area. Thank goodness, she hadn't noticed me behind her.

When we reached the parking area, I paused and watched as she walked toward a car. Just as I suspected. It was the car that had been behind me. My heart beat faster. What would I do now? Karla got something out of the car. Instead of coming back my way, she headed toward the festival area. I had to check out that car and make sure it was the exact one. Would I find the hat that she'd worn?

Now that she had stepped away, I rushed over to the car. No one was around the vehicle, but I had to make sure that it stayed that way. I didn't want to get caught snooping. Once I reached the car, I scanned the surroundings, trying to act casual. I yawned. I checked the time on my watch. Was I being too obvious? Perhaps. With no one watching, I stepped up closer to the car and peered inside. It was a mess inside.

I noticed the camera sitting right there on the seat. I reached out and tried the door handle. The car was unlocked. Did I dare pick the camera up and take a gander? If anyone saw me, they would think that I was trying to take the camera. How would I explain that to Pierce or Caleb. I supposed that was a chance I'd have to take because I was too curious to let this opportunity pass me by.

With my heart beating faster and my legs shaking, I opened the car door. I hurried and grabbed the camera. The name on the camera shocked me. Mark. What was his camera doing in this car? I knew little about cameras, so I hoped that I wouldn't mess this up or do the wrong thing. But they were all alike, right? I hoped. I pushed on the POWER button, and the screen popped up with pictures. I moved the little arrow button and scrolled through.

The first photos were of a red car. I'd never seen it before. I scrolled through to the next pictures. Flowers. How sweet. He didn't seem like he would be interested in flowers as the subject for his pictures. Next were tree and landscape photos. But the next photo I recognized right away. A photo of the river. The same river where Erica had been found. My fear grew as I studied the photo. This guy had been to the river.

When I got to the next photo, my heart skipped a beat. I surveyed the surroundings to see if anybody was watching. Still no one was around. I needed to show this evidence to Caleb and Pierce, but I couldn't take the camera.

Erica was in the photo at the river. And even worse, it appeared that she was wearing the same clothing as the day I had found her body. The photo was taken at the scene of the crime when Erica had been murdered. There had to be a way to get the date from this photo. That would prove the exact time it had been taken.

Needless to say, I was excited about what I'd found. I had to take a photo of this camera and the screen for proof. Setting the camera on the hood of the car, I pulled out my phone. This could be the thing that solved the case. After snapping a photo, I hurried and put the camera back on the seat just as I'd found it.

I felt as if I might be running out of time. Now what would I do with this information? I had to hurry back to the trailer so that I could call Pierce and Caleb. Which one to call first? It was Pierce's case, so I would have to call him, although doing that would probably make Caleb feel left out. Surely, he would understand. Yes, he was a professional, and I knew he would understand.

When I got back to my trailer, I took Van in my arms, pulled out my phone, and dialed Pierce's number.

"Pick up, pick up," I said.

Unfortunately, my call went to his voice mail. I hadn't planned on that. Now what would I do? My plan B would be to call Caleb. I felt as if someone needed to know about this immediately.

Movement caught my attention, and I thought it was Ama's grandpa. He was over by the wooded path, probably still hoping that Ama would follow him and go back to the other dimension. It hadn't happened so far, and I doubted she would do it now.

Van jumped from my arms and took off running toward Grandpa. I screamed out for Van to stop, but he didn't listen. He ran for Grandpa with all his energy. Van was lightning-fast, and I wasn't sure I would be able to catch him. Usually, he never did stuff like this. Nevertheless, I ran after him, all the while yelling at him to stop. Unfortunately, he wasn't listening to me. I had hoped maybe he would stop when he reached Grandpa. When Grandpa headed farther down the path, I knew that Van would continue to pursue him.

Ama yelled for her grandfather to stop as she ran behind me. We reached the path, and I tried to keep my footing as I yelled for Van to stop. Once at the river, Grandpa and Van stopped. I tried to catch my breath.

"Why did you do that, Van?" I asked.

Ama was behind me. "Why did you do that, Grandpa?"

Before the grandfather had a chance to respond, a noise came from over my shoulder. My breath caught in my throat, and my heart sped up. I spun around, hoping to find the source of the sound. Movement caught my attention. I spotted Mark as he stepped out from behind one of the nearby trees. It felt as if someone had punched me in the stomach. I was having a hard time breathing. So it was him after all.

Mark had just successfully lured me back here to the scene of the crime. And I would inevitably meet the same fate as Erica. Without uttering a word, he raced toward me. I tried to run over and grab Van because there was no way I would leave him behind. Even in a case of life or death.

Maybe we should jump in the river. Could I swim with him to safety? No, that was definitely a bad idea. I wasn't a good swimmer. My only hope was to get down that path and back to the fair area, where someone might see us. However, I didn't get a chance to reach Van before Mark caught up with me. He wrapped his arms around me and pulled me backward until I fell onto the ground. Now he was on top of me. His hands were wrapped around my neck.

Why was he doing this, and how would I save myself? It seemed impossible to break away. Van was biting Mark's ankle, but it didn't seem to faze him at all. What would happen to Van once I was gone? Would Mark attack the dog for biting his ankle? Ama screamed for someone to help. But unless there was another psychic around, no one was going to hear her. I checked around, trying to think of something that would get Mark off me.

My hands clawed at the dirt underneath me as he tightened his hold on my neck. The pain was terrible as I struggled to breath. I scanned my surroundings, hoping that maybe I would find something to grab and possibly hit him with it.

Maybe that would lessen his grip on my neck enough for me to get away.

My hand made contact with glass. When I glanced down, I saw that I had found a bottle. A bottle of root beer, nonetheless. Thank goodness, Danny had been out here again littering. That was not normally something I would say, but I was so thankful. My hand was wrapped around the bottle's neck. Now I had one chance at smashing Mark over the head with it. If this didn't work, there would be nothing else.

With all my strength, I swung my arm with the bottle, making contact on Mark's head. It did the trick. He fell off me immediately and tumbled to the ground, clutching his head. I managed to scramble up from the ground. Van was already on the path, waiting for me, as if he knew that we were going to run.

"Get out of here," Ama screamed. "Before he gets up and grabs you again."

I ran as fast as I could to the path. I headed down it with Van running behind me. All of a sudden, I smacked right into someone's chest. My gaze traveled up, and I realized Pierce was right in front of me.

"What's going on?" he asked.

I pointed at Mark as he tried to get up from the ground. "He's the one who killed Erica, and he was just trying to strangle me. I smashed him in the head with the root beer bottle."

"Stay right here," Pierce said.

He took off down the path toward Mark with his gun pulled. I watched in stunned silence as

Pierce pulled Mark up from the ground. Pierce had Mark in handcuffs within ten seconds.

"What's happening, Celeste?" Caleb asked from over my shoulder.

I spun around and realized that he'd just walked up. "Pierce just arrested Mark for killing Erica. He tried to kill me too."

"What are you doing out here?" Caleb asked.

Now was not the time for asking questions like that.

"It's a long story . . ." I released a deep breath.

"I'm willing to wait," Caleb said.

"Van ran out down the path, and I was trying to catch him. The next thing I knew, Mark was here too, and he was trying to strangle me."

"How did you get away?"

"Danny's trash. He left another bottle. Well, I assume he was the one who left the bottle."

"I'm just so glad you're all right." Caleb embraced me in a hug.

Pierce was walking up the path, guiding Mark toward us. I didn't want to face Mark again. Terrifying thoughts filled my mind when I remembered how close I'd come to being strangled.

"My, that was scary, Celeste. With your quick thinking, you saved yourself. I'm happy that you're all right." Ama scowled at Grandpa. "It's all his fault for luring you back here to begin with."

"Don't be too hard on him. He had no way of knowing this would happen. He was just trying to get you to go back to the other side."

Van sat at my feet. I scooped him up and hugged him tightly. Caleb and I followed Pierce down the path as he led Mark away. Thank goodness, this was over. Now everyone could feel safe again.

We reached the end of the path and spilled back into the fair area. Activities were still going on as usual. No one had a clue what had just happened down by the river, though it didn't take long for people to notice that Pierce was leading Mark out in handcuffs.

People were stopping to watch the scene. Police cars had arrived in the parking area now. Sirens wailed, and flashing lights swirled. Ama and her grandfather walked behind me. I just hoped that I would be able to help them resolve their argument. Caleb and I stepped just to the edge of the parking lot and watched Pierce as he stuffed Mark into the police car. In the back seat of the cruiser, Mark rocked from side to side, thrashing around as if trying to escape the handcuffs. A shiver raced down my spine.

"I can't believe this happened," Caleb said. "Wait. I should believe it. You worked really hard to find the killer. You're an excellent sleuth, Celeste Cabot."

CHAPTER 26

*After the event, remember to calculate
your profit. Don't panic if you had a loss.
You'll do better next time. Maybe a ghost
will help you.*

"I'm relieved that's over," Ama said.

"Me too," I said, forgetting that the others couldn't see her.

At first, everyone around seemed confused, but I supposed some of them remembered that I sometimes had ghosts hanging around.

"Well, now that that's over, I think we should leave," Grandpa said.

"No, I think that we still have unfinished business here," Ama said.

What could that unfinished business possibly be? Though I didn't want to burst her bubble and tell her I thought everything had been solved.

"I've put up with this long enough now. I think it's time for you to come back with me," Grandpa said.

Ama crossed her arms in front of her chest, as if pouting. "I'm not going anywhere."

I really had to do something to bring these two together.

"If you guys will excuse me for a minute, I need to speak with the ghosts."

Caleb gestured with a wave of his hand.

Pierce winked. "Sure, go right ahead."

"You guys can come with me." I motioned.

Grandpa scowled but ultimately came with me. Ama was still pouting, with her arms crossed in front of her. Nevertheless, she came along with me too. I had no idea what I was going to say to them. But I had to get these two together.

"Where should we go to talk?" I whispered. "Maybe that nearby oak tree."

Ama and Grandpa shrugged. "Fine, the oak tree it is."

Once at the large tree, I kept my front facing the tree so that no one would notice me talking, although I was sure that facing the tree seemed strange enough to anyone who was watching. They probably thought I was completely nuts. Lucky for me, though, everyone was still paying attention to the police presence, so I would probably go unnoticed for a while.

"Okay, what can I do to get you two together? I want you to get along. After all, you're family, and I know you love each other. What do you say? Shouldn't you all make up now?"

"It seems like you want to get rid of me," Ama said.

"No, absolutely not. I love having you around, but I imagine you have other things that you need to take care of on the other side. You seem like kind of a guardian angel, and I think someone else might need your help."

"I know no one needs her help on this side," Grandpa said. "We just need her to come back to the other side."

Okay, clearly this wasn't working. I had to think of something else. The two were at an impasse, staring at each other and unwilling to budge. And I was caught in the middle. Telling Ama that I didn't want her here would hurt her feelings, so that wasn't an option. And I enjoyed her company, but I knew it wasn't right for her to stay around. She was stubborn, just like her grandfather, though.

Suddenly, I realized Ama was becoming more and more see-through. I wasn't seeing her as a complete living person. Now she appeared sheer, like a projected image. Ama must have noticed my strange reaction.

"What's wrong, Celeste?" she asked.

"I can see right through you."

Ama peered down at her hands and saw what was happening.

"What's happening?" A revelation came across her face. "Oh . . . I know what's wrong."

"What's wrong?" I asked.

"Now that I've helped you, it's time for me to go back. I'm not strong now. I need to go back and recharge my energy. I'm fading fast."

Grandpa tossed up his hands. "Thank you. It's about time I got you to leave. Now it's time that you go."

"Not so fast. I have to say good-bye to Celeste

first. I'll be back to see you, Celeste. I promise. This isn't really good-bye. It's only good-bye for now."

"I hope this isn't good-bye. You take care, okay?"

"Don't worry about me. You take care of yourself. You're always getting into trouble."

She'd barely finished the sentence when, right before my eyes, she disappeared. I spun around to see if Grandpa had disappeared as well. Yes, he was gone too. They'd gone back to the other dimension in a blink of the eye. Poof . . . they'd disappeared. I didn't get a chance to say a proper good-bye.

I raced around to the other side of the tree, hoping I'd find them there. Sadly, there was no sign of them. I'd wanted them to go because I knew that was the right thing, but now I was sad.

"Celeste, are you all right?" Caleb's voice carried through the air and around the tree.

When I stepped back around, I found Caleb standing there. I knew I looked quite frazzled.

"The ghosts are gone," I said.

"Well, that's a good thing, right? You wanted them to leave?"

I released a deep breath. "Yes, but I thought I'd get a little more time before they left."

"How do you know they're gone?" he asked.

"I was talking to Ama when all of a sudden she began to fade. Poof, she was gone. Grandpa left with her."

"Did they go back to the other dimension?" Caleb asked.

"I don't know for sure if they did, but I think their time and energy here ran out."

"Well, I suppose she wanted to help you, and that's exactly what she did. So that's why she was able to leave. I'm sure once they're in the other dimension, they'll work out things between them."

"She said that, once she's saved up enough energy, she might reappear," I said.

"Well, at least you'll know how to deal with them if they come back," he said.

When I checked across the way, I spotted Pierce. After a couple of seconds, he headed our way. Now the two men stood beside each other.

"Did you get things worked out?" I asked.

"I don't know if Pierce and I will ever have things worked out, as you say," Caleb said.

I placed my hands on my hips. "I think you guys could be really good friends."

"I don't know about that," Pierce said.

"You have a lot of things in common."

They eyed each other up and down.

"Like what?" Caleb asked.

"Oh, I don't know . . . investigating murders."

"That's probably about all."

"What will it take for me to get you together?" I motioned for the men to follow me.

They walked behind me as we headed back over toward the festival. My parents stood with my brothers. Of course, my brothers were showing off their trophies for coming in first and second in the hot dog eating contest. Just as we reached everyone, Sammie rushed up.

Sammie grabbed me in a hug. "Oh, my gosh,

Celeste, I heard what happened. How are you?
Have you calmed down? Did he hurt you?"

"I'm not hurt, but I think it'll take a while for
me to calm down."

"Are you sure you're all right?" She touched
my neck, checking for injuries. "I mean, that was
a pretty traumatic thing that happened."

I waved off her concern. "I'll be just fine. At
least, the killer is going to jail."

We focused on the police car. Officers moved
around the scene. Festivalgoers waited for more
action from the cops.

"Mark's going to jail, thanks to Celeste and
Van," Caleb said.

"And the ghosts—which, by the way, are no
longer here."

"They left?" Sammie asked with wide eyes.
"Wow. Well, I'm just glad that you're all right."

"Don't worry about me. I'll be just fine as
long as I can paint and I have Van."

"And as long as she can investigate murders,"
Pierce said with a wink.

We watched as the police car with Mark in the
back pulled away. Karla had been staring in shock
at the entire scene. I supposed it was just a coincidence that she was here at the craft fair at the
same time as Erica. I wasn't even sure that Erica
had been aware that Karla was here. As for
Danny? Well, the fact that he was a litterbug had
saved me. Without that bottle, I would have never
been able to hit Mark over the head. I wouldn't
have been able to get away.

"Maybe I need to offer Danny a thank-you for
leaving that bottle by the river," I said.

"How about you give him a thank-you gift of some more root beer?" Caleb said.

"I like that idea. Though I'm pretty sure he'd be suspicious of anything I gave him. He's just a little strange but ultimately harmless, I suppose."

I'd been almost convinced Danny was the killer for a long time. Until I'd found the camera with the photos of the river and saw Erica wearing the exact same clothing from the day of the murder. Then I knew that I'd found the killer.

Movement out of the corner of my eye caught my attention. Karla was rushing away from the festival. The memory popped into my head. How had I almost forgotten? She had gone to Mark's car. Plus, she had followed me. I didn't have answers as to why she'd done this.

I hurried over to Pierce and touched his arm to capture his attention. "Karla followed me. I meant to tell you. Plus, I found the camera in Mark's car with the photos. She went to his car as well and got something out of it. She was extremely comfortable getting into his car, like they knew each other. I think she might be involved."

I pointed in her direction. She noticed my movement and ran. Pierce sprinted away toward Karla. In another second, Caleb ran after him.

I stood with my family as we watched the scene unfold. Soon Pierce had reached Karla. She spun around, facing him. She acted as if she might actually lunge at him. I could've told her that wasn't a good idea. Caleb approached at that point. They stood in front of her, waiting for her next move. Pierce must've said something to Karla because she held her hands up. Pierce moved toward Karla. Next, she placed her hands behind her back. Within seconds, Pierce had her in handcuffs.

"Wow, that was something to behold," Stevie said.

"And you wonder why I worry about you," my mother said.

"It is dangerous," Sammie said.

"You're not helping," I said with a shake of my head.

"Well, it's the truth," Sammy added.

Pierce guided Karla over to another police car. They'd arrested her in less than ten minutes.

"Well, I believe this is proof that you should have avoided this festival," my father said. "I told her to stay away from this place, but she never listens to me. She's just like her mother."

My mother rolled her eyes. Caleb walked back over to us.

"What happened?" I asked.

"Pierce confronted her with the information you'd given him."

"What did she say?" Sammie asked.

"She basically confessed that Mark and she had conspired to commit the crime," Caleb said.

"But why would they do this? I mean, why would they want to do that? I can see why Karla had a motive. What about Mark?" I asked.

"Mark is a disturbed individual, obviously. Karla paid him money because she wanted to get rid of Erica."

"Well, that makes sense. I can't believe that she admitted it," I said.

"I think the pressure of it all made her snap," Caleb said.

One of the creepy clowns had walked up to us now. He was dancing, trying to make us laugh. Obviously, the clown had no idea what we'd just been through. I supposed he was trying to make us feel better.

"Now are you ready to go?" my father asked.

The craziness wasn't over, though. Across the busy festival area, I spotted the person who had been hiding behind the tree earlier. At the time, I thought maybe it had been Karla, but now I recognized something about the woman, and I knew who this was instantly. Gold bangle bracelets were visible, dangling from underneath the sleeve of her black blouse.

"What is Madame Gerard doing here?" I asked.

Everyone followed the direction of my pointing finger.

Caleb squinted to see from the bright sunshine. "That is her."

"I'm going to go find out why she's here." I left everyone and headed her way.

When she realized that I was walking toward her, she tried to get away.

"Madame Gerard," I yelled out.

She didn't pay attention, or if she had heard

me, she wasn't responding. She moved swiftly, so I had to pick up my pace. Soon I was short of breath from my sprint, but ultimately, I reached her. When I touched her arm, a chill raced across my body. I hadn't expected that reaction. Madame Gerard stopped and faced me. She removed her big black sunglasses.

The hat and sunglasses had been the reason why I'd thought that Karla had been the one behind the tree.

"Madame Gerard, I'm surprised to see you here," I said.

"I imagine you are," she said.

"Why are you here?" I asked, hoping she would answer.

"Well, to be honest, I've done some snooping on my own. I wanted to find the person who broke into my home." She held her head up high. "Ultimately, I chased him back to this festival. I watched as the police officers arrested him. I'm kind of proud of myself."

"Mark was the one who broke into your place?"

"Yes, it was him. I'm sure of it," she said.

"Why would he do that?" I asked.

"I suppose he saw you coming to my place and thought that I could offer some information on whether or not you were close to finding the killer."

"How did you track him down? How did you know he's the one who was in your house?"

"I'm psychic, dear." She put on her sunglasses again. "Plus, when I was working in the garden today, I found his wallet. I went to his address and followed him here. I still say I'm a good sleuth, though."

A bubble of laughter exploded within me as I said, "Yes, Madame Gerard, you make a great detective."

Her lips twitched before a low melodic chortle escaped her. Madame Gerard had actually shown emotion. That was what I called a happy ending.

ACKNOWLEDGMENTS

Many thanks to my family and friends. They embrace my quirkiness. Love you all! Also, thank you to my editor, Michaela Hamilton, and my agent, Jill Marsal.

Don't miss the next delightful Haunted Craft
Fair mystery by Rose Pressey

MURDER CAN HAUNT YOUR HANDIWORK
Coming soon from
Kensington Publishing Corp.

CHAPTER 1

A loud crash echoed across the expanse of the massive room. Screams soon followed. Somehow, I knew the sounds were related to my brothers and/or my father. They were always in the middle of some chaos or other. If something destructive happened near them, they were typically somehow involved.

I dashed around the corner and saw my brother Stevie standing behind the red velvet barrier rope. The space had been blocked off so that tourists would know to stay out. Either my brother chose to ignore the rope and the "KEEP OUT" warning signs or he truly was clueless. Honestly, I thought he was just kind of oblivious. My brothers never meant harm. They just lived in their own little world.

My other brother, Hank, stood behind the rope barrier too. Which one had knocked over the vase? Unfortunately, I knew the large ceramic urn had to be an expensive piece of artwork. Why else would it be featured on top of a pedestal column at the Biltmore Estate unless it was pricey and had significant importance. Yes, my brothers were a walking disaster. It was no wonder, though. Their clumsiness combined with their muscular physiques was the right mix for disaster.

My family and I were currently touring the magnificent mansion. That included my mother, father, grandmother, and two brothers. Now I questioned why I had agreed to come along with them for the tour. Obviously, I'd been wrong when I'd thought they could behave themselves for just a few minutes.

My petite, gray-haired grandmother stood a good distance away from us, clinging to her brown pocketbook as if she might have to make a quick escape. That was probably good thinking on her part. This wasn't her first rodeo with this bunch.

My mother clutched her pearl necklace as if the jewelry would save her from fainting. I'd picked out the necklace, which my father had given her for their thirtieth anniversary. She'd pretended she believed he'd chosen the pearls, but she'd winked at me, indicating that she thought I'd made a perfect selection. Sometimes when I saw my mother, it was like seeing my own reflection. The resemblance was uncanny; her dark hair and big brown eyes, like mine, were the shade of one of my favorite things—decadent chocolate.

"I don't know how I managed to get through thirty years of this much chaos," my mother said.

My father was at a different attraction. With the same strong stature as my brothers—although with a bit of added cushion—my father would inevitably get into trouble around breakables. He lifted the rope and scurried under to the other side. The extra weight around his middle made the movement not as easy for him as it would have been years ago, but he still managed to slide underneath.

"Mom!" I pointed.

"Oh, for Pete's sake, Eddie," she said as she ran over him. "Get out from behind there before they arrest you."

"Why would they arrest me? They put the stuff here for us to enjoy, right?" My father reached out and grabbed another vase.

Since I'd known him all my life, I understood what he'd said, but others had a hard time deciphering his low, mumbled words. Of course, as I suspected would happen, within seconds the priceless piece slipped from my father's fingers. My mother dove for the item as if she was the star player in a baseball game trying to catch the ball. This all played out in slow motion. At least, that was the way it seemed in my mind. My mother caught the vase as she plunged to the floor. A groan escaped her lips as she rolled onto her side with the expensive item still firmly in her arms. Gasps filled the once-silent room.

After a few seconds, my mother lifted the vase. "Got it!"

"Score," Hank yelled.

As my father helped my mother to her feet, I ran over and grabbed the vase before he had a chance to get his hands on it again.

Employees raced over with stunned expressions on their faces. I kind of wanted to just run the other way because I didn't want them to know I was involved. Since I now held the valuable piece of art, I supposed it would be hard to act as if I wasn't related to these people. My brothers laughed from somewhere behind me. The male employee narrowed his eye and marched over to me.

He yanked the vase from my arms. "Please step out from behind the rope."

The woman motioned for my mother and father to move as well. Yes, a trip to the Biltmore Estate had definitely been a bad idea. What once had promised to be a lovely afternoon was now a complete disaster. I grabbed one of my brothers and yanked him to the side.

"What?" he said with a chuckle. "It was an honest mistake. Dad probably thought this was a flea market and was searching for a price tag."

"Why were you on the other side of that rope too?" I asked. "I can't take you all anywhere."

"You never take me anywhere," he said.

"Now you know why," I said.

Yes, technically my family had invited themselves on this trip. They'd followed me all the way from Gatlinburg.

Stevie sauntered over to my side. "We just wanted to get a better view of the fancy-schmancy stuff. You can't blame us for that."

"Yes, I can blame you for that," I said in a louder voice than I'd intended.

"We're going to have to ask you all to please exit." The tall, muscular, bald-headed man gestured toward the door.

The word SECURITY was written in big white letters across the front of his black shirt.

"Oh no, I didn't get to see everything," my mother said in a pouty tone.

"Is it really necessary that we leave?" my father asked.

The man stared blankly at my father.

"He wants to know if it's necessary that we leave," I said. "We'll be good."

The man gestured toward the door again, giving my father the answer without saying a word.

"Okay, I think it's best if we just leave." I looped my arm through my mother's and guided her toward the door.

Glancing back, I realized my father was standing there, staring at the mural on the ceiling. I rushed over and yanked him to come along with me. Everyone in the room stared at us. It was more attention than I wanted. My father and brothers reluctantly obeyed and marched behind us.

"Sorry," I said over my shoulder at the employees.

Frustration covered their faces, as if they wanted no part of my apology. I totally understood their point of view. Plus, my bank account couldn't afford to reimburse the estate if one of my wacky relatives broke something else. Being asked to leave was a blessing in disguise.

My family and I walked past the groups of tourists entering the estate. They looked as if they were having a delightful time. With my family, I realized serenity wasn't in the cards for me. Bright sunshine surrounded us as we stepped out of the estate. I blinked, trying to adjust to the light. A vast array of colors surrounded us; the lawns were lush and the trees full of green leaves. The assortment of trees included magnolia, cherry, and crabapple, to name just a few. Pink hyacinths, yellow daffodils, and red tulips bloomed around the space. It was so much to take in that I felt I'd never see it all.

"Well, thanks to you all, we almost got arrested for damaging property or trespassing or who knows what else," I said. "Thank goodness, I saved you from going to jail. Once again. It's like that time you all decided to work on Mr. Renfrow's car without telling him."

"We had to test-drive the Cadillac to see if it was fixed. If we'd told him, it would have ruined the surprise," Stevie said with a crocked smile.

"I saved you from being arrested that time too. Just like now," I said, with a point of my finger.

"Why would you say that you saved us? What did we do?" Stevie asked with a frown.

"She got you out of there without causing any more damage," my mother said. "You all nearly broke two things."

I motioned for my family to quicken their steps as we marched toward the parking area. With any luck, I'd convince them to go home. Not that I didn't love my family, but with their natural knack of creating chaos, I felt I owed it to everyone to keep them away. I was staying behind because I'd signed up to be a part of the Fifth Annual Fall Biltmore Estate Craft Fair being held on the grounds. I couldn't have been happier about the upcoming event. If my family stayed, I knew something disastrous would happen. It would be like throwing a wet canvas tarp over my beautiful art.

I hoped to sell quite a few of my paintings while here. Each time I signed Celeste Cabot to the bottom of a painting, my heart danced. I took pride in signing my name to each one, since now I was a full-time painter. Recently, I'd quit my job at my Aunt Patsy's diner back in Gatlinburg and decided to chase my dreams. Never had I thought I'd have this opportunity. I knew it wouldn't be easy, but I was giving it my best shot.

As soon as my family left, I'd head over to the perimeter of the estate, where the craft fair was to be held. Tomorrow was the first day, and I had a lot to do before the first customers arrived. Not only did my paintings have to be ready, but I had to finish last-minute tasks too. There was a lot more to a craft fair than just providing the items to sell.

"Well, good-bye, everyone, it's been a lot of fun," I said with a wave.

"She's being sarcastic now," Stevie said.

"You're right about that," I said.

"Don't be too mad at them, Celeste. They didn't mean to do anything," my mother said as she patted Stevie and Hank on the back.

She was always defending them. That was partly why they acted this way. They were always getting into some kind of trouble, and my mother ignored their behavior. And my father was generally either setting fire to something accidentally or injuring himself, sometimes both. Stevie and Hank always broke things, including their bones. The anarchy would never end. One by one, I hugged them all and said good-bye.

"Thanks for coming, you all. I'll see you back at home," I said.

"Oh, we'll be back to help you later," my mother said with a smile. "Your father needs to eat and take a nap."

It was as if she was taking care of a toddler.

"What do you mean? Aren't you going back to Gatlinburg now?" I asked with panic in my voice.

Suddenly my chest felt tighter. My surroundings spun ever so slightly. I felt it was hard to breathe. They hopped in my mom's blue Buick. My mother lowered the window.

"We'll be around tomorrow, dear. We haven't seen all of the estate either. This is our vacation. See you," she said with a wave.

"Yeah, there's a lot more to do," Stevie said around a chuckle.

"Yes, we have to see more, I suppose," my father mumbled.

My family usually relayed my father's messages to others. Stevie and Hank smiled, and my father said something that I didn't understand this time. I supposed I wasn't one hundred percent fluent in his mumbling. I sighed and waved good-bye as the Buick pulled away with a slight squeal of the tires. Of course, people walking around the area all noticed when my family made their grand departure.

I wanted to hide behind the nearest pine tree. Nevertheless, there was no time for that. They'd already scrutinized me, possibly wondering if I had an answer as to why my family was so boisterous. I had no answer for that. Instead, I waved and smiled, trying to indicate that everything was just peachy. At least, I'd get a bit of calm before the family storm returned. For now, I was on my way to my latest adventure. Nothing would wipe the smile from my face right now.

Even if I managed to convince my family to head home, I wouldn't be alone at the craft fair this week. I had my wonderful friend Vincent van Gogh. My four-pound chihuahua was my constant companion. I called him Van for short. People would say I rescued him from the shelter, but in reality, he had rescued me. I'd named him Van because he had one ear that flopped over, making it appear as if it was missing. Plus, my obvious love of art had spurred the moniker too.

My 1947 pink Ford -F100 truck and my adorable, pink-and-white Shasta trailer were parked just down the way. That was where I'd set up my art to sell tomorrow. Van was asleep in the trailer, waiting for me to return.

When I reached into my pocket, I realized my keys weren't there. Panic set in right away. Where had I lost them? This had better not be another one of my brothers' practical jokes, like the time they stole my sneakers from gym class and I'd had to walk home barefoot. I had to find them soon, or I'd have to call a locksmith to open the trailer.

I bet I'd lost them inside the mansion. Would they allow me back in to search for them? Probably not. Maybe they already had posters of my family plastered around with a no-entry warning. Nevertheless, I had to try. I ran back over to the area where we'd been kicked out only a short time ago.

A middle-aged, brown-haired woman stood at the door when I approached. She eyed me up and down. She narrowed her eyes. No doubt she recognized me.

I pulled out the ticket stub. "I think I lost my keys inside. Do you mind if I go inside and check?"

She shrugged and motioned for me to go inside. I hadn't expected that. She didn't even so much as touch my ticket stub. I didn't mention this, though. If I pointed that out, she might change her mind. I hurried inside the mansion. People spoke in hushed tones in the distance. What would I do if the other employees recognized me? I supposed I'd deal with that when it happened.

With anxiety churning in my stomach, I walked down the hallway. I tried to hold my head high as if I was totally supposed to be here. I'd almost made it to the area where the vase incident happened. I figured this was the location where I'd lost the keys. As I made my way farther down the hall, a piercing scream rang out. What had happened? Had my family returned? That wasn't possible, right? The next thing I knew, a stampede of people raced toward me. Since I knew I was slow and wouldn't be able to keep up with the group, I dove to my left so that I wouldn't be trampled.

I landed face first on the floor, but not before knocking down one of those velvet rope barriers that I had just chastised my brothers about being behind. For a brief time, I remained motionless, dazed and wondering what had just happened. The crowd thundered by like a herd of cattle without saying a word to me. Apparently, they just wanted out.

I managed to get up from the floor. After straightening my clothing and smoothing down my frazzled hair, I picked up the gold posts holding the barrier rope. Curiosity got the better of me, and I really wanted to take a peek around the corner and see what the crowd could've possibly been running from. I didn't smell smoke, nor did I hear a fire alarm. What other emergency could there have been? With one quick glance around the corner, I saw the motionless woman on the floor.

Grab These Cozy Mysteries
from
Kensington Books

Nail-Biting Romantic Suspense
from Your Favorite Authors